Dedication

With prayers of healing
for the transforming Earth

To my daughter with appreciation for your
rare and real creative spirit.

For Aysha Love,
in recognition of your bravery
to never back down.

For Aysha's family, with enormous respect
for their long years of dedication
to birth the seeds of consciousness.

With love for all those unacknowledged souls
baring the birth pains of this new humanity.

Acknowledgments

To Aysha Love without whose wisdom this text could not exist, for years of love and support, editing and mentoring.

To Holiday Geiger for her bright spirit, enormous generosity and faith.

To John and Marcia Perkins for believing in me and forging a real alternative.

For the sisterhood who have sustained me and the wondrous men who are stepping up.

To my dear Mexican friends of Baja, California and my fellow writers through the long years learning together.

Preface

With the turning of the millennium we have been forced to deal with crisis and disasters that thunder ceaselessly to shake us loose from our barriers of non-communication. As an ever more vocal, growing mass of humanity stirs from complacency, we hunger to remake the world in love, to melt the generational ice frozen in our weary hearts. I have learned from a remarkable woman, who was my mentor for thirty years that we can create a new inner wholeness to respond compassionately to the call of life. But, it will require total personal responsibility at every level. This woman taught me that it is ours to awaken a radical new diligence and intense self-awareness, to weave a new world out of the matrix of misery we have spun. And, to do so we will have to learn how to create an emotional continuity of care.

This brave feminine genius taught me that to give birth to a global humanitarian response and make the evolutionary leap out of the emotional distortions and barbarism of the past we will have to face ourselves squarely, journey into the core of our buried emotions found in the Deep Shadow Self and release power's hold on our present and therefore, the future.

Einstein's famous "Insanity is doing the same thing over and over again expecting a different result" becomes our keynote.

Through my relationship with this woman, Aysha Love, the Creator of Emotional Quantum Intelligence, I was blessed with years of love, support and truth through the crisis of my own dark night. She challenged me and showed me the way to break my addictions to power. Shining a light on the structure, the emotion, and energy of my Deep Shadow Self a real path of care finally broke through. My journey with Aysha has become the 'prima materia' of <u>Stealing the Moon</u>.

Like Natalie in <u>Stealing the Moon</u> my first real look at those struggling with inner darkness was in my youth, before I meet Aysha, from the inside of a mental ward. It was there I prayed that I might one day be able to impact our pathetic approach to healing the mentally ill. I saw how modern science is completely baffled in the face of this tragedy and, in the name of helping people stages a mass abandonment of those suffering from these 'curses of the mind.' After undergoing years of therapy including psychoanalysis, and myriad traditional and alternative approaches then finally Primal Therapy, I had a clear idea of my inner terrain but nothing substantial had shifted.

I met Aysha when she was founder of Bridge Mountain, one of the world's first growth centers for human potential development.

At that time I had become a Primal-based therapist myself, administering over 6000 hours of regression sessions with clients at my fifteen-acre ranch/center, Steppingstone, in San Rafael, California. I midwifed many people through the traumas of birth and childhood's primal pain. I was there as they resurfaced deep trauma that overwhelmed them, shutting down their willingness to feel for a lifetime. Over and over again after so much wrenching catharsis I experienced that they were no more responsive or caring than before they lay down their thousands of dollars in the hopes of finding the 'cure for neurosis.'

The inadequacy of all the many therapies I had voyaged through including Primal became more blatant the fateful summer Aysha arrived at Steppingstone. She worked with each of my struggling clients, helping them move beyond their blocks into a whole new embrace of life. It was a summer of astounding breakthroughs! I was shown something real could be done to augment the beginnings of emotional health. At the same time I was confronted with my own limitations. I could only bring people to where I had actually gotten to myself! And, more troubling, something within me seemed to be opposing their healing. I, like Natalie in <u>Stealing the Moon</u> terminated my practice and joined Aysha at the Castle where she lived and worked in Spain. That was thirty years ago.

<u>Stealing the Moon</u> was born of the emotional healing and confrontation with the Deep Shadow Self I was lucky enough to have received engaging in Aysha's Emotional Quantum Intelligence process.

Aysha was one of our true unacknowledged divine feminine avatars, a western woman who charted a path of emotional self-healing like no other before her.

In <u>Stealing the Moon</u> I have been given the privilege to embody Aysha through the character of Shemura. To some Aysha was a love goddess, like Shemura in <u>Stealing the Moon</u>. But it was her insistence on being a real woman who loved life and was aware of the structure and emotional energies in the collective unconscious matrix that made her a true revolutionary for our souls, shifting everyone she touched with her love and commitment to life out of the deadlock of time. Of course the totality of Aysha's presence and her work is far beyond what I have been able to portray. Her creative feminine genius, her sensuality, light, humor, ego less gentle presence, and transcendent cosmic feminine consciousness lifted all that knew her. Her ceaseless bravery unmasked the hidden unconscious agendas of power. Her eternal innocence, birthed unparalleled transformation in all she touched. Aysha's comprehension of how to transform the Deep Shadow Self and restore the damaged divine feminine potential is the plasma I have gladly drawn upon to bring my characters alive.

Working with leaders in the arts, politics and education over long years of service, Aysha charted a radical new perception of the Archetypes of the Collective Unconscious, confronting and cleansing their emotional corruption from a perverted take over by mankind's addiction to power. She freed up enormous complex energies locked in the collective matrix making way for the future.

Stealing the Moon is a voyage into what happened to the vast suppressed divine feminine potential. Its purpose is to give an experience of woman's quest to alchemize that enormous energy into the fuel for global commitment to the often difficult, painful and yet ultimately liberating process of taking deep personal responsibility for ones emotions, thoughts and actions.

On January 3, 2004 Aysha crossed over. The vacuum her parting leaves is enormous. But within that loss, she has planted the seeds of consciousness that grow within us daily.

Luckily for those who did not benefit from knowing her directly, she formed an organization called Sensorium which now intends to give the wealth of her gifts, including her plethora of unpublished books, a video library of her journey into the Archetypes, and many other creative tools to help humanity rebirth love into the core of our lives. Sensorium will be the platform to launch all this. Aysha worked with me designing seminars to surface and heal the Deep Shadow Self. I am honored to say these 'Shadowland' seminars plus the 'Righting Our Lives' intensives described in the last chapter of this text will be hosted by Sensorium. Sensorium's website and my own can be found at the end of this book.

Before Aysha crossed over she mentored me patiently over ten years, editing voluminous rewrites of this and two other books. Stealing the Moon has emerged as the first in that series. It is a work of creative non-fiction, fiction based on fact. Its revelations about Ancient Egypt, with its expose of the relationship of Nefertiti, Akenhaten and their daughters all came through the direct experience of Aysha, myself and the women, children and men who lived and worked with her. The contents of this heretofore-unknown emotional history surfaced synchronistically over a period of years. Gradually the pieces came together making up the landscape of that time and its implications to the present. It was a group dynamic that unearthed this hidden emotional truth of an epic still having an enormous impact on humanity today.

Please understand, that all the characters in <u>Stealing the Moon</u> are fictitious; composite pieces of real people and actual events re orchestrated to render deeper truths. It is true that Shemura is drawn as a partial rendering of Aysha's presence and wisdom. Also, there are parallels between Natalie and Nefertiti's interwoven lives and my own. Regardless, I have taken the liberty to creatively cut and paste together parts of the whole into a tapestry that I hope, is at once compelling and clear. Nevertheless, make no mistake; <u>Stealing the Moon</u> is a real expose, filled with core truth. It is my deep wish that it's telling wound no one. None of the characters represent the real life of any one person living or dead.

May <u>Stealing the Moon</u> assist you in purging the nightmare of the 'Deep Shadow Self'. May our children never have to pass this way again. May it help to forge open the gates of unconscious emotional controls and free cloaked awareness. May it nourish the seeds of loving action and care within the beauty of Emotional Quantum Intelligence.

Contents

Chapter

1

My back was turned when my patient set fire to his hands. He must have wrapped them in the tissue I kept for teary-eyed patients and then grabbed for my lighter. He was going to be my first brilliant success 'down under'. I, Dr. Natalie Stearn, feminist American Psychologist was going to revolutionize New Zealand's Mental Health System. A radiant healer of immeasurable love, my mentor Shemura had just won a research grant after dazzling the Viennese psychoanalyst's convention with her miraculous results. She left Freud's apostles howling at the moon; curing psychosis with touch, compassion and her radical discovery of the field of Emotional Intelligence! I had followed her abroad possessed by an unnamed obsession to be her next protégé.

After Europe we traveled around the world, meeting impassioned women everywhere, ready to unfasten the corsets of patriarchal restraint. Generations of bottled up wisdom were about to catapult a worldwide change. She was central to it, birthing a new psychology wedding science to soul, ushering in love as the missing link.

Because of her, the Kingsgate Psychiatric Hospital trusted me with Riley, their long-term psychotic who spoke only in gibberish. He was an awkward adolescent who ambled backwards nervously hiding in his private world of nonsense rhymes. Once they took him off his medication the tidal wave of his past abuse begged for expression. For two days and nights I cradled him as he transited torture.

We were raw with his psyche's labor pains, shaming the regular staff that prayed our round the clock vigil was not to be in their future.

After 72 hours he spoke his first coherent words of a lifetime.

"Don't you come near me you son of a bitch. You bastard, I'll never let you hurt me again" he shouted, his eyes staring straight into mine. I loved every syllable of his foul-mouthed declaration of independence. Freedom's ring was sweet, even if it did chime out with profanity.

He was a different person after that, speaking quietly, his steady eyes determined to brave the riptides of terror that had held him mute. Like a newborn, he lay in my arms, opening himself heroically to the sensations of his restored life.

Then, when we had unlocked this total tenderness he so deeply needed, I felt an indescribable energy rise up in my body, like a fiery beast hungry for ages. I wanted to feast on his fresh innocence, to fill myself with his purity. He saw the horrific hunger in my eyes. It was enough to make him retreat back into his vacant world.

This is not what happened when Shemura healed. She turned herself even more into a love-being. I had wanted to devour him. Never in my life had I felt something so evil. My betrayal drenched him in blood and incest, returning him to the nightmare of his father's lust. As I turned to escape the full impact of what I had done he lit himself on fire.

2

His screams of anguish filled the ward.

"Oh Christ, he's burning up," the security guard shouted, breaking in and dousing the boy with fire retardant. Then the nurses injected him with a horse strength tranquilizer, but it did nothing to quell his unimaginable pain. His departing stare bore a hole in my life of unexplored depths. In the hopes of discovering to what purpose I'd turned into this dark goddess. I shut down my practice and returned to the states. This manuscript is the chronicle of my investigation.

Chapter

2

The Shambhala Lodge, Las Madrinas, Arizona April, 2004

It took me a week of blurred arrangements to withdraw from my life as a psychologist. Las Madrinas, Arizona, wasn't my first choice. Morocco would have been more exciting, losing myself to its maze of ancient medinas, inhaling air luscious with sandalwood and musk, cloaking myself in the colorful Berber tribal women's silver and gold weaved jalabahs. Overwhelmed with the desire to flee what I had to face, I dreamed of disappearing behind their veils, to bask with them in invisibility.

Las Madrinas lent me another sort of invisibility with its seductive offer of sanctuary. And if it was selling divine bliss to harried tourists for top dollar I was at least, in the beginning, innocent of the conspiracy. A letter arrived at my New Zealand flat perfectly timed to provide the way out. Inside were two tickets, pre-booked by one of my spiritually minded colleagues. I was to attend a weekend seminar at the Shambhala Lodge, dedicated to the illumination of the human spirit. All that was left for me to do was to extend my stay indefinitely.

The Shambhala lodge hung precariously off sand cliffs that lined the regions red rock canyon. It reminded me of a reclining phallus of domed glass on top of an adobe fortress. Inside it's enormous hall I felt intimidated, eyed by Archangel Michael whose portrait rode the filigreed cathedral ceiling. Two steps inside and I was blinded by the light show of a hundred tilt-a- whirl crystal prisms. After my sixteen-hour flight from Auckland I wanted darkness. I barked at the turbaned concierge to "Hurry for God's sake." with my caravan of trunks bursting with volumes of old journals and my unfinished novel. He reminded me that everything in the Shambhala hundred acre reserve was 'for the sake of God' and asked me if I hadn't been informed that I was entering a sacred vortex.

Before I could answer, a scurrying cluster of yoga students assaulted me. Their smiles reflected those crystals unbearable glare. After they ran my Visa through, I was shown into the Grand Solarium where potted palms drooped over pyramids of vegetarian burritos laying in a sickly sauce. I didn't want lunch. I wanted to hide in my room, afraid my head would burst, like a cracked watermelon spitting soggy seeds of castigation onto their spotless Persian carpets.

I cursed, bumping into a mob of blissed-out revelers, while the program director pitched the upcoming Festival of Light to be hosted by their latest western heir apparent of eastern mysticism, Guru Yogicar.

Giant candles were being lit next to the gargantuan fireplace. Paper boats signifying the sojourn to Nirvana where bobbing up against those blinding crystals. Their exuberant spinning was making me nauseous. Tipping the concierge, I backed into my room unable to shake off the sensation I had landed in the Super Bowl of Enlightenment. How would I survive ensconced in this mob of pie-eyed mystics? I looked at the room that was to be my home until I birthed myself free from these feelings of evil. I snubbed the décor, it's prefabricated glass coffee table, the futon divan, the two basket armchairs, the macramé hung plants and, imitation Indian carpet. They were all coordinated in non-committal pastels. The thought of living alone suffocated by their generic tone sent me into a panic. But where else could I go? There was nothing but desert from here to the airport. Staring into the mirrored bathroom wall I barely recognized the shifty aging Jewess that glared back me.

Sinking into the king-sized waterbed I closed my eyes to slow the assault of memory, but the phone rang.

"Natalie" I heard my name called from the other side of the world. "The clinic has burned."

"But the fire was completely out when I left. How could that be?"

"I don't know. It couldn't have been Riley. He's in real bad shape. They have him sedated and cuffed to his burn bed, in solitary. There's nothing left Natalie. Hal and Terry are accusing you of witchcraft. It is odd that it happened the very night you expressed such regret, insisting you had to terminate your career for this bizarre calling, this spiritual purification or whatever. No one seriously holds you responsible for Riley. It happens to all of us at least once in our illustrious careers. You didn't need to leave over one relapse, even if you did see 'Whirlwinds of dark energy spiraling up from your interior.' I don't believe in any of your woo woo stuff, not for a minute. You're way to hard on yourself Natalie. We all feel guilty when one of our patients doesn't make it. It happens to the best of us."

"Nigel, the clinic, there's nothing left? Was anyone else hurt?" I asked dumbfounded by his news.

"No, they were all back in the dorm. It's all our records, the files and Natalie, your research project, your documentation of Shemura's work, it's all gone."

I could barely listen as he told me to stay as long as I needed, that they were all moving into portables. Hanging up, I felt the devastation I had created explode in my blood, carrying emptiness through my jet-lagged bones. I had destroyed Riley's chance for a descent life and with it Shemura's reputation. Breaking into a sweat, I pulled back the patio doors insisting the night air fan me with its coolness. Sitting up all night, I dissolved, shaking with fear as owls screeched and bats fluttered across the red rock canyon. By morning my lips were blue with frost, as the orange and purple dawn paled into a bleached sun of self-condemnation.

All morning the lines to New Zealand were busy. When I finally got through to Shemura her voice was soft and comforting as I made my confession.

" We're all hurting with Riley." She said. I was sure she was going to chide me for assaulting her research but she was too upset about the boy whose life I had threatened.

"I've seen this in you from the beginning, Natalie," she said responding to my confession.

"I thought your pursuit of the work would have brought you through the door by now, but it hasn't. Riley was so special so brave. I am hoping we can reverse some of the damage." She paused, as though she were taking a silent moment to lend strength to his wounded spirit. Then her voice changed with a strange determination.

"You're about to become a voyager into the forbidden world of the female unconscious mind. You are going to stay, until you resolve this, within yourself aren't you?" She asked.

I whispered "Yes" as her concern filled me with gratitude and loss.

She advised me to keep a safe distance from herself, and her extended family of real and adopted children.

"I don't know if I would have recommended Las Madrinas," Shemura went on. "It's a formidable earth energy vortex. The acceleration of light there will draw out of you rapid-fire paranormal phenomena." I could tell she was still watching out for me, even as her career lay in ruins.

"Will it be dangerous?" I asked, frightened by the sudden alarm in her usually relaxed voice.

"If this is what I think it is, there may be real danger. I'd send one of us to be with you but I can't take the risk even though I know we are what you will miss the most."

She was right. She had helped her children carve themselves from the fabric of complacency with knives of dedication. They were all hard working harbingers of care unacknowledged modern day saints. Their joyous giving natures and courageous poetic souls were living proof Shemura's breakthrough in Emotional Intelligence could create a different genre of homo sapien worthy of the name human.

"Maybe it is for the best you are there." She went on evaluating every angle of my circumstance.

" The vortex will help you find the roots of this and pull it up to the surface, if you're willing to face yourself head on and stop the denial."

"How do you mean?" I asked.

"The vortex will dredge it from your depths. The triggers of women like yourself, who chose perversion, live in your cellular memory. The vortex will act like a time tunnel because of the earth's immense healing force there. Pray, meditate, and listen. Give everything to this if it is truly what you want." She paused and I could feel her sensing deep into the vortex as though there were no distance between us.

"It's going to be like you're on a mind expanding drug at times there. People interact on vortexes as though they have known each other forever. As you journey, weeks can span lifetimes."

"Journey? Into what?" I asked pushing back panic. "How can I believe anything if it's going to be like a drug?"

"Because it's not a drug. It's life pulling out of you what keeps you from being a person whose presence others can trust. Whatever is against a harmony with nature will no longer be able to exist. Vortexes are do or die places. You're upping the ante just being there."

"I've always had you by my side. You've always been my

cover. Now I've damaged your name, your work. How can I ever make this up to you?" I asked, my throat tightening against my loss.

"Work until you are satisfied your female spirit is beginning to direct your life, not your contracts with power."

"What are my contracts with power Shemura, do you know?"

"Yes, I think so but it won't do you any good for me to hold your hand this time. You need to excavate your own strength, it's the only way. Many are impacted by the actions of a few. Learn what piece of the story is yours and tell it."

"Tell it?" I asked grabbing for her words like a rope to pull me from quicksand.

"You are going to be writing aren't you? Life and your creativity will find a way. Let me know how it's going."

When she hung up I realized how addicted I had become to having her near. But why? Why would a grown woman need another woman with so much desperation? I didn't have the answer. I only knew I had never been more alone.

Unable to move, I lay for hours in my bed drifting backwards, to sixteen, to madness, to the mental hospital where I had abandoned myself to suicide, long before Shemura lit my life with hope. The sad child I had been was calling me back. How could I comfort her now when I did not know the origin of this perversion that lived within us both? I tried to rest but couldn't dislodge the vision of Riley's burning hands. I was out of excuses. I had to make the effort to track this internal violence to its source.

Chapter

3

I sat on my patio all the next day with my cape covering me, like a criminal hiding from prosecution in a foreign land. As night closed in I paced the hotel corridor. The sci-fi channel blared, echoing from behind the row of closed doors. Separated from any other human life, explosions of loneliness tore at me. I pulled open the emergency doors and ducked out onto the Shambhala reserve. A river waved eerily in the opal moonlight. The moon was rising, turning the desert into a maze of shadows. Driven for what seemed like hours, I wandered aimlessly, eventually stumbling, twisting my ankle on the embankment's jagged rocks. It was then I spotted a circle of enormous stones, sitting like a ring of tribal women gathered to weather eternity. As I walked towards them a cave opened before me, like a crack between the toes of a boulder goddess. Its intimidating darkness frightened me until a mysterious compassion poured over me, breaking the shell of my aloneness. Yielding to the magnetism I went inside. There was only enough room to lay with my arms folded, crossed over my breasts, just like a mummy. A chill washed over me as I remembered Shemura's warning, "The vortex is a time tunnel of immense healing force."

The chill turned to a biting cold, freezing my flesh. As I searched for warmth the room turned golden as though someone had lit the chamber in candlelight. Shadows caste elaborate jeweled designs surrounding me in a carousel of ancient artistry that could only be Egyptian. Long-neck cranes and graceful striding elk were chiseled amongst hieroglyphs on the cave's walls. Amulets and vases danced in the golden light.

Then with a horrible gush, ice-cold water flooded past me. It was as though a dam had burst from somewhere deep inside the earth releasing a torrent to the surface driving me out. As I fled I heard these words.

"It's a play held in your genes. You won't be free until it is written Nefertiti."

Drenched, I limped like a nearly drowned animal along the river's embankment, back to Shambhala. Coughing into the night air my head spun with questions. Nefertiti? A play? What play? I was no playwright!

Back in my room I pulled my saturated sweater dress over my soggy wedge of Hebraic curls and stepped into the shower. I let the warm water wash away the night's chill. It took a quarter hour until my body finally began to calm.

Sighing with relief I slid inside the rose satin sheets. Almost lost to sleep I was jolted awake when disturbing bantering figures jeered at me the very same way they had back in New Zealand! I had grown so upset with them I phoned Nigel to collect someone, anyone, a psychic or priest. I didn't care so long as they came at once to cleanse my flat of this nuisance. The psychic told me they were spirits who had died in my old Victorian flat and for a donation he would rid me of them forever. But here they were again! I tore myself from the comfort of my bed, grabbed a vase and hurled it at them. Their mayhem solidified into a singular mask. It glared at me with anonymous hostile eyes then barraged me with a pain so profound I was thrown from my body. My spirit was sent banging down a passageway lined in oblong skulls.

"Really Nefertiti, you didn't expect me to let you do this all alone now did you?" The mask chided, pursuing me as my spirit crashed into the very same chilling cave from which I had just returned. The chamber staled with rotted vermin and mold but, there was no mistaking it this time. I was inside an Egyptian tomb of death and treasures allotted to the privileged. I lit by the gold sarcophagus carved with the symbols to guarantee eternity as an intimacy engulfed me. Raising my hands I begged to be freed from what was consuming my life.

The mask came at me, churning itself with a bitter wind that burned my dislodged spirit. Then it formed into a ghoulish swell, drawing up my life of frustrated desire. I did nothing to resist as the ghoul undressed my hunger uniting me with an enormous zeal. It became a phallus that sank deep into me, arousing my infant deprivation then strained down my spirit throat, overwhelming all restraint. I was famine hungering to be taken. Its cold blistering currents whipped me in hypnotic rhythms until my only prayer was to be filled with its ghoulish release. Etheric hands puppeteered my disembodied spirit nipples, growing them hard under a masterful command. I stiffened, begging for it's inhuman force to end my misery. My orgasm burst with a gaseous venom, like an overfull cyst. Then the ghoul fed upon my release, like a child slurps the bottom of a melted sundae.

I screamed in protest at what I had allowed. The screams of my remorse drove me back to my body. I knelt by the patio railing my heart cramped with revulsion. The moon burst through the starless sky. I prayed for understanding as the moon's gentle rays lifted me from perversions grip into a shimmering love. Bathed in the grace of moonlight the suffering, the aloneness, disappeared! I felt thoroughly loved, thoroughly comforted. From out of the rays of moonlight crystal tones caressed me:

"Daughter of tarnished light. Lift up your gaze. What has

13

become of my children? Where are my true ones? Who has silenced the good women devoted to my fire? Why have they not co-authored the world in which you now live? Where are my temples that brought their kindness and truth to enlighten worldly flesh? Why have men stopped cleansing their selfish mindless actions through the portal these divine women's love? Go to the child within, the one you abandoned on the mind priest's couch. Learn what bitter fruit binds you to perversion."

Then like an abandoned lover shook from bliss I was alone, watching the morning sun command the new sky; feeling myself of no more pure intent than a desert fox ready to stalk anything moving for a morsel of vitality.

Chapter

4

All morning a harsh wind pelted the spring desert flowers bruising their gleaming faces. I took the service elevator to breakfast. When I returned, under my door I found a note from Hal informing me Riley had been released from the burn unit. The damage was extensive; he was virtually catatonic. An investigation was being launched into Shemura's work. My mistreatment of the poor boy was blocking her ability to carry on her crusade of care.

After the bellhop delivered my groceries, I turned off the phone, drew the shutters closed, and read the journal of my tangled child's life. On the way to the shower I glimpsed my face in the mirrored bathroom wall. As I stared at my reflection a coned crown began to form on the top of my head. I could not move as my cranium elongated. I no longer recognized the person before me. I ran to the phone switched on the line and watched dumbly as my hands dialed Shemura's number. Her voice was sweet and clear as a chapel bell.

"I don't know how I can ask for your help now," I pleaded, "I got the news about Riley and the investigation. If circumstances were reversed I'd cut you from my life like a tumor." I waited for Shemura to do just that but she remained calm encouraging me to explain the details of my visions. Reluctantly I divulged my debauch with the ghoul to Shemura.

"In the mirror my face is no longer my own. My head is elongating and I am wearing a strange cone shaped crown. It has a ribbon of colors inlaid around the edge. In the cave the voice called me Nefertiti. It's her, isn't it? Great! Every mad women thinks she's Cleopatra or some renowned Queen of The World. Why not Nefertiti?" I asked in a mesh of fear and disbelief. She responded in her usual open relaxed tone, "People are fascinated by 'past lives' but they don't really understand how it all works yet. Past lives are inadequate descriptions of how souls carry their stories from existence to existence anyway. Did you know that many souls can be patterned by the blueprint of key figures in history they know nothing about? The impact of their lifetimes can anonymously spread across nationalities, even epochs like seedpods. Try to talk about that on the morning show," she joked.

"Why is Nefertiti appearing in my mirror? What should I do with her?" I asked, wishing a simple explanation could return normalcy back to my upside down life.

"Nothing. You're not directing the course of this healing; the spiritual force inherent in life is doing that job. If it's time for Nefertiti to speak it will happen somehow, if not, she won't. First things first. Your own past must be screaming in your ears by now. Until you experience that for what it was you're not going any deeper. This all depends on how thorough you're willing to be, Natalie, how committed! Pick up the magnifying glass and examine your own life from your earliest recollection. Trust that you will be taken where you need to go."

As she went on I could not help comparing Shemura's mercy in continuing to help me with the generosity she attributed to life itself.

"Reconstruct the events of your early life using your remote viewing skills if you like, but don't be surprised if it goes another way," she advised mysteriously.

"Another way? What way? If this is not my past life then what is it? I don't understand," I persisted shamelessly.

"It may be and it may not. If you let fear lock you in you won't get anything done. It could be you're not the only soul that carries the memory of the Queen of Egypt but for some reason the information is being released through you. It's possible your affiliation with me makes you a prime candidate to bring it out so the world can benefit. It really doesn't matter. Record your direct experience. Have you ever studied Egyptian magic?" she asked.

"No, never, should I have?" I responded, choked with fright.

"Not necessarily. Maybe it's best you know nothing. Become the Sherlock Holmes of your own memory banks. Sound interesting?" she asked laughing as I broke into a cold sweat. As we talked, I watched the wind and rain form into tiny funnel clouds pelting the shutters on my patio windows, like monster hummingbirds waiting to be fed.

"Blowing up a storm there is it?" Shemura volunteered being present on both ends of the call simultaneously as only she could.

"It's like a tormented spirit trying to beat its way through the shutters into my room, so I've made sure to latch all the windows shut."

"Maybe when this is over you won't let the wind get away from you like that," she joked.

"What do you mean? I have something to do with this wind?"

"When women reclaim their relationship to divinity, what transformation the world will witness then! The energy of the ancient goddesses and their priestesses didn't just evaporate without trace. Let's not forget Einstein? Remember, energy can neither be created nor destroyed?"

"What are you saying? The wind has something to do with my female force getting away from me? What does that have to do with Nefertiti?" I asked, ashamed of my demanding tone.

"If people only knew the shenanigans that go on in the invisible realms of their own psyches. Thank heavens it's starting to come out at last. Humanity is ready to reclaim its birthright. Each one of us is a player connected to the sacred mysteries by an invisible field of energy. The mystics call it the God within, the Indians include it in their understanding of the Great Spirit, and the humanists see it as a matrix of human potential. Even science has a name for it now, the morphogenic field. Carl Jung discovered it almost a century ago calling it the collective unconscious. Nothing could change much until the collective curiosity could bust apart some antiquated assumptions" Shemura continued, further explaining her paradigm. "What is the make-up of our unconscious mind? Who are we to believe? All western theories of the mind have opposing views and were conceived by men, many of whom had very troubled emotional natures. How are we going to heal if we continue to operate out of their constructs? Be brave! Do something that only a few women have done before. Investigate your own female psyche and record your findings. Your connection to me and my work, along with the vortex, should be enough to surface things quickly. You're not alone. There is help all around you." Her voice trailed off suddenly as a child called her name.

"I have to go now. Taris is having another bout of trouble with my grandson. You don't know anything about that do you?" she asked impishly.

"No, how could I from here? I'm sorry, I really am but what could that have to do with me?" I asked.

"Maybe we'll find answers to questions we didn't even know we had.

Mora called, she is doing well but I can feel underneath she continues to struggle. Have you spoken to her lately?" she questioned. Mora, my daughter and I rarely communicated.

"No," I answered reluctantly, "We still talk on our birthdays but that's it."

"Maybe you'll find an answer to that as well. Ok then Sherlock, don't forget your intuition can be the voice of the soul inspired by life whispering in your ear. Tally ho!" As we hung up her voice, like a smile, clung sweetly to my lips.

I made a cup of chamomile tea and parted the shutters. Replaying our conversation my panic calmed, but nothing made any real sense. I could hardly believe this woman, whose reputation I had damaged so severely, could be so light-hearted with me.

As fits of sand and wind lashed at the slightly opened shutters I was reminded of the Kingsgate Hospital fire. If some disassociated energy of mine could be kicking up the desert sand was it possible that it could have set Kingsgate on fire half way round the world? If so, was it tied to a queen I knew nothing about? I searched my memory for any recollection of Nefertiti. All I could recall was her bust sold at tourist stores I had visited while on vacation.

I sat in prayer all day until the storm settled. As the setting sun sautéed the bland décor with butterfly speckles of golden light I had the feeling I was being watched by eyes floating through space, like two sinister intruders, breaking in on my pleas for clarity and healing. Determined not to be distracted, I resolved to reconstruct the events of my early life. I would use my remote viewing skills to relive what had to be faced. I had been trained extensively and was confident I could tape record an accurate regression session with my voice sensitive headgear.

I called the front desk to hold my calls, put out dried apricots, figs and nuts by my bed, then parted the shutters slightly. The first stars of evening lit my quilt in a celestial tapestry. As I counted myself down a voice of beautiful crystal tones broke in re-directing me down another inner highway. "Explore your child's need as it soured distorting all future womanly pursuit. When the goddess cultures flourished, women formed a loving support around each of their young girls as they made their delicate and volatile transition into womanhood. Their female force protected her as she took her own virginity, letting loose her first blood. This assured that no other person would possess her. This is as is should be. Female sexuality was seen as a sacrament, a gift from the goddess, to be used in sacred ritual uniting lovers with the wonders of divine creation. Now it is time to uncover the rituals that formed women like you for another purpose."

When I asked who was speaking, the crystal voice spoke softly with gentle authority. "I am the Earth, I am your mother, I am life." I lay in silence, left to initiate what I set out to do by my own determination. Resuming to count myself down, tape recorder in hand, I am hopeful the clues to the predator I have become will reveal themselves. I feel a hot thirsty breath on the back of my neck, trying to distract me, from penetrating the illicit gaps in my perceptions. Mute eyes that have suffered great loss flash mournfully before me and then quickly fade as I return to the winter of 1964.

Transcript of Dr. Natalie Stearn
Session One

Regression back to the Evansville Psychiatric Hospital
Evansville, Illinois January 9, 1964

At sixteen, a bottle of sleeping pills was my ticket to the madhouse. I used pills to dissolve my holocaust interior. My mother finds me, two days later wrapped in sweat and vomit, and calls for the experts. For the next week I stared out with indifference from behind iron bars, waiting for the modern gods of the mind to make themselves known, not wanting to admit they already had. My mind was being evaluated by those trained in the science of no emotional response.

After my week of solitary confinement, I am allowed to re-enter the world. I sit in the group room beside a boy who dizzies me with eyes like two spinning blades. He speaks in riddles, like Riley, pleasing himself that he is undetectable. I live alongside Adele, an ex-1940's Miss Wisconsin. Her dangling flesh is an etheric white nightmare. Thin pasty skin sagged and quivering with lost beauty cover paper-thin bones. She floats in and out holding her pink nightgown modestly closed, as if someone would leave her standing naked. She lets go only to fiddle with her lank grey hair, or to reapply candy apple lip-gloss to her once breathtaking lips.

Medication is her ringmaster. Through the day I hear she is married to a man that strips her dignity, she hustles tables in his grease kitchen while upstairs he bangs the hired help. She hears the springs on their bed, like a crown of thorns pounding above her head while she waits his tables. She fries bacon and mops floors to his deep breathing. He always looks forward to getting her pregnant. With clockwork precision, always a month from her due date, he forces himself upon her. She is rushed to the hospital where they try to save her babies. But he won't stop at the hospital door. He keeps coming into her room until he bangs out a whole litter of still born babes. Not one of her children survives. "Why is it important for me to remember her now?"

My roommate, a schoolteacher of thirty years, returns, from Electro-convulsive therapy. She is crying, begging for someone to help her. She turns towards me.

"Do you know my name?" she begs. I do nothing to help her. I am consumed in private victory, tying the Dot candy box I smuggled in, to my neon overhead light. The ward is a homeless barracks decorated with female shrapnel.

"If you say that one more time, I'll go mad" chides Edith, her cigarette hanging off the corner of her wrinkled mouth. She draws meager laughter from the throats of our strangled group room.

"Shut up would you," she bellows at the boy drooling to his own logarithms. "Your gonna drive me crazy" she chortles, bringing on another wave of tear-faced laughter. Edith has eight sons. Dutiful mother to her army nine months of the year, she vacations with yearly bouts of insanity. Usually she threatens to kill one of them. It always gets her back here where she is unofficially in charge of this group of people who won't answer back. Communing with our madhouse full of broken humpty dumpties she is right at home, hanging out with the unloved.

We sit around all day playing dominos or rummy. Orderlies with their eyes at half-mast dispense medication while our white flags of surrender blow in their objective faces. We are swaddled dropouts no longer running the upwardly mobile racing track. We have all cracked from exhaustion racing towards the 'American Dream.' It is a relief to be souls with disenfranchised bodies. We are no longer worthy to slay each other for illusions. No longer encouraged along the path of greed and materialism. We hang our garments in the nut house closet. With my attempted suicide I have reenlisted in some ancient legion of the undead. I do not know whom I serve wearing my robes of no self-identity. I grow comfortable with this new freedom to sit blank faced; nothing asked of me but that I look crazy.

Regression back to one week later

Panic is my morning light. I wake to my roommate's screams. The sleep deprived medical students announce their blank faced authority. They hold no instrument to remove the wedge I have driven with my suicide between the living and myself. With rote good mornings they probe me, aborting the winds of healing that wipe the tears from my embarrassed adolescent face. I cloak my need for help.

"I did this to myself," is all I feel safe enough to say. And then I let it slip, "There are these voices. They spar for my devotion. One is beautiful. But I can't make it out. If only I could hear it clearly, I swear I wouldn't need to be here anymore, I'd know what to do."

Facial smirks, then vigorous note taking detach me from my simple plea. They leave now, whispering into tape recorders. The psychiatrist calls my mother. He tells her that her child is broken. It will cost thousands to repair me. In-depth psychoanalysis is my only hope. Hearing voices, even barely audible whispers, meant to roust the soul are signs of grave mental illness.

The Amtrak home is a fighting mob of heated nostrils. Commuters steam the windows with frustration, soaked in the worst blizzard of the decade. Painted in winter ornaments of ice I enter my mother's suburban kitchen. Smoking, she doesn't look up. "How can you do this to your own mother?" she asks me.

I run upstairs to my bedroom and double bolt my door against the fear that without thinking I will rush to strangle her. I do not see that underneath her accusations, she too is begging for mercy.

By night she is yelling at my door. "You're killing me. I can't cope with you anymore, your confusion, you don't try, you're not sincere. I can't do the impossible. You are so immature self-centered, unrealistic, unwilling to make compromises. I'm bowing out. I'm too weak and fragile to cope with this awful situation. Let the professionals handle you. Hoodwink who ever you can. No one is going to do this to me again! I've been used and used up enough in this life. Go, see an analyst, you need one!"

My psychoanalyst's office is downtown, an hour's ride on the Amtrak, buried between rows of businessmen. I am to see this guy three times a week. My mother and I are told curing me could take years, possibly a decade. Staring out the window snow continues to pile and drift, erasing miles of crewcut lawns.

Behind my newspaper I mourn the lost comfort of never again living as an ordinary person.

Flying up his escalator too fast to keep my breath, I believe at the top of the tower there is a man who will help me heal. In his antechamber I pray he will refund me to the negotiable world, teach me the skills to inhabit my life, help me to end my stay in the junkyard for wash-away Jewish princesses, become a blessing on my mother's house.

My sweaty fingerprints are sticky with implausibility. When he finally opens his door I stand before a man fully gray. His skin is pallid, his eyes underscored in bags bloated with the homelessness of souls he has listened to through years of cool detachment. Sigmund Freud's portrait hangs over his slate head. I feel the father of modern psychiatry fix his gaze upon me as I walk about searching for a chair. The analyst instructs me to lie on his divan and to say everything that comes into my mind. Freud's apostle leans into his cushioned chair and takes up his tablet. My body stiffens as I take up my position on his divan. I fight it with all I have in me but it is as if I am caught between two opposing intents. I want this man's powerful healing to be my miracle, to help me build the force that will vanquish what has grown morbid in my female heart.

Time responds to my need. I am back at my birth! Stiff men wash my blood from their hands. My newborn flesh is stung with separation from all that is holy, profound and even the presence of my mother is denied. My incubator motor hums piping in artificial air that keeps me alive, yet also drowns out the celestial music that plays for all children.

"Be my mother," I plead to the nurses wheeling me back to the nursery. Only the monitors respond, bleeping and flashing their programmed crimson light, bathing me in a "Pepto Bismo" glare. My brand new ears ache with the whispers of starched men repeating "staph infection and quarantine."

I am wheeled by my mother's bedside. She is my first one-night stand. Starved for her nurturing touch, I nurse on her thoughts and emotions, drawing them in with an ancient psychic power. Her fearful memories of World War II and the Great Depression are my first supper.

I will take anything into me, but it is almost impossible to find sustenance. I am the rain on my Mama's parade. My insides contract in arrhythmic fits. I burn for her breasts to sooth my raw intestines. I am forming my psyche out of my Mama's frustration as her spirit swirls into mine. We drift past her dreams of admiring men, her slender long sexy legs and Ester Williams smile tossed in her very own, fully paid for, dream pool salad. She wants to be treated like a queen, and so do I. She is a powerhouse of thwarted potential. I jump deeper into my Mama's mind suckling her "Woolworth" bubble-bath fantasy. She wants to be admired for her singing talents, to be someone important.

Horowitz, my psychoanalyst insists, "A newborn is incapable of taking into herself her mother's psyche from the incubator." We are both convinced, but I cannot stop suckling on my Mama's pain and longing.

She does not want anyone to call her "big tits" anymore or laugh at her full breasts. She slumps and wears trench coats in the Chicago summer heat to avoid the gangs of boys waiting with their jeering laughter. She hates the very breasts I'm craving. She hates being a woman, and so do I. I break out in diaper rash memories mourning my mother's humiliated breasts. Horowitz says I'm avoiding something more important but he doesn't give hints.

A cold thing has come to help me in the incubator. At first I don't tell Horowitz. It covers my eyes from the full extent of my Mommy's resentment for my toxic birth and the forty pounds she put on because of me. I kick it away and latch onto her singing talent. I am stuck to her, longing to be a 40's diva. Her song sticks to the back of my throat:

Enjoy yourself, it's later than you think.
Enjoy yourself, while your still in the pink
The years go by, as quickly as a wink,
So enjoy yourself, enjoy yourself,
It's later than you think.

Her unsung melody becomes a groan. It pushes me down until I cannot outrun the cold thing that hunts me scurrying inside my baby's body. She is my groaner. Someone just for me. I love her light denying hold. I let her become my sickly bodies carrying case. My groaner inhabits the space where I have abandoned myself. I am sucked into her sick oblivion that is my first earthly home. Her sour notes quell my pain, allowing me to fall into my first deep child's sleep.

When I awake my mother is gone, doctor's orders. She is resting on the sleeper train bound for the Borsht Belt. For some reason, the men of science have encouraged the only person who holds the key to busting me out of my "plastic bubble" to also abandon me entirely.

Three weeks pass before my doctor breaks the seal on my incubator. I am sent home to a sociopathic nurse who ropes my brother to his bed leaving him to defecate on himself, she strolls me barely clad, to her boyfriends place during my first Chicago blizzard.

My parents are told by the neighbors to come home at once. But I have already let my groaner drive hopelessness, depression, panic and fear deep into me. I am addicted to her numbing clasp. Wrapped in the groaner's dark embrace the light burns me. I nuzzle deeper into her. She is my happy hag of warts and broken veins and I refuse to realize her bulky threat. Appendages torn in fits of uncontrollable bitterness collect on cobwebbed shelves. She should not be in my body at all. She thinks she is helping. Neither of us wants to admit she is consuming my humanness or that I want her to.

Horowitz says I made up the groaner. Psychic possession is not real. He insists there is nothing that could do that inside a baby.

"Babies are not conscious nor capable of such realities." I was a girl with an overactive imagination, making up supernatural stories. Embellishing the routine birth of a little Jewish girl with an unfortunate staph infection in the late 1940's, on the south side of Chicago.

Chapter

5

Regression Session Two
I return to April 1964 Chicago, Illinois
As my Psychoanalysis continues

It's springtime. I want something to bust me out of my incubator walls right here on his couch. Horowitz's chipboard ceiling is dissolving into my mother's immaculately groomed lawn. After dark, she floods the backyard with neon, searching for weeds like a prison guard patrolling for a jailbreak. The next day is Easter Sunday. We are Jewish but we celebrate any holiday that lets us shop. I run outside looking for the bunny. My brother leaps out of my mother's squared off lilac hedge. Our summer bodies wrestle somewhere between best friends and fierce competitors. We play cowgirl and Indian, hiding from my mother in our camping tent turned tee-pee. I imagine a wise big chief squinting, with penetrating eyes, giving me his sound advice, "Horowitz is no chocolate egg!"

My analyst taps his ballpoint as ballsy crocuses bust through blocks of ice, encouraging me. I am intoxicated, remembering the smells of our dwarf apple tree. Drunk on her sexy perfume as it splashes it's morning lilac and lemon up to my bedroom window. I need Horowitz to come back with me into the yawning fifties, into Westland Park, our fledgling suburb not yet sprawl enough to overcome acres of naked forest. I will paint him with its uncontrollable foliage. I will bring the color back to his pallid jowls.

"Come with me, dear doctor, into my childhood of wildflower fields and dirt roads, far from your Chicago, your boxing arena of swollen feet. Come float with me out on Lake Michigan. Let's bob on summer waters, far from my mother's coffee klatch of gossiping friends. Let our surf washed bodies ripple into two ghastly raisins running to shore, shrieking for our lives."

He reprimands my desire calling it "transference." I am trying to turn him into what I can never have, love.

"Just say whatever comes into your mind, ignore anyone is in the room with you at all," he explains.

His refusal fuels my willfulness. He will hide with me under the spawning Oaks. I want Freud's man to invent plays with me the same way I dragged my girlfriends onto my backyard stage to take my directions. I want him to thrill to my made up sonnets, stick pins into stolen tulips on my mother's Sears and Roebuck sheets, be my best friend.

"Let's fill our mouths with the sweetness of fresh baked sugar cookies, then wash them down together with the tartness of tree-ripened lemonade" I beg my doctor.

He writes. Frustration tugs up past addiction, filling me with fresh obsession. I want him to bind my heart back into my nervous rolling chest. Why won't he give anything? Why do I believe in his power more than the muffled voice I have shredded my life to retrieve?

I am only certain of one thing. As the gift of healing is offered to me I lay it upon his alter, for his strangling reinterpretation, sacrificing it up to his indifference. All the while protesting, determined not to be so easily dismissed. There must be other psychoanalysts who are not as frozen, why was he chosen for me?

Unable to stop myself I am a babe again before him. I describe myself crawling out to my mother's vegetable garden, diapers down to my knees. I pull onions up from the moist earth, eating them by the handfuls. Their spindly roots tickle my belly.

My brave hunter brother, Ralph, captures a flying squad of monarchs with his thirteenth-birthday-present net. Our basement throbs with a hundred butterfly wings. We burst our sides laughing as Aunt Lilly runs up the rumpus room stairs screaming "Oye gevalt."

Not even a cough comes from Horowitz. I jump into cornucopias of cool autumn harvest divesting myself of summer's heavy heat. The waxen gold of leaves piled with relief wait to burst in the red glow of well-tended neighborhood bon-fires.

Horowitz is silent.

Swinging my flaming roasted marshmallow torch in his face I shout "Scaramouch" playing musketeers with my uncle. We run with lit jack-o-lanterns across the suburban night scaring our zombie neighbors away from their television rituals of sedation.

Horowitz's silence runs over my need to heal. Why won't I open my eyes and stamp him with deserved enemy status? Why do I beacon him in deeper?

"Come doctor. Imagine a winter safe for small children to wander home alone in the dark, snowflakes forming harlequin masks on roused checks. Feel the rapture of Shelton's French fries, how Nestle chocolate comforts frostbitten lips. Watch our skirts fly on elementary school blacktop, transformed into a dancehall of opal ice. Be happy for me, kissing my first beau inside the bamboo thicket turned into a forest of glass reflection.

He commands me to ignore his presence entirely. I take a vow of silence, spending weeks wasting my mother's money, refusing to speak. He does not stop writing. Is he catching up on correspondence? No. He stands at the top of the temple. He will come around in time to reunite my breath with life. It is his century.

Chapter

6

Regression session three, May 1964

I rock on his analyst's couch watching Horowitz's room
steal light from the setting sun. Looking to offset gloom
I run to greet the memory of my daddy. I am a pink crinoline
wall of bouncing fluff. I blow soap bubbles to caress his bristly
moustache. He holds his sore back and schleps his big sacks
down the rumpus room stairs. After the ball game he invites my
uncle over and in front of our gaudy Chinese flowered drapes I
become my daddy's little teapot. My uncle loves my little handle
and my little spout and how I get all steamed up and shout,

"Tip me over and pour me out."

I'm pouring to make my daddy happy. Why is he taking my
mother's bags from the hospital out to his car? He is steadying
her staph infected body with his big strong arms. He's leaving
me in the incubator and going with her on vacation. No, I protest,
it can't be true. My daddy would never take my mama away and
leave me to the groaner. Why would he do that to me?

33

"It wasn't his fault." I tell Horowitz. "He did what the doctors told him to do. He was a good man, a good provider."

I won't let anything destroy my singular shrine of childhood love.

"He fought for thirty years to keep food on our table." I tell Horowitz. "He came home to us every weekend fighting Wisconsin's snow and Minnesota's black ice highways." I insist. "The road broke his back, put him in the hospital, but he never missed a week-end."

I want to stay with the memory of my good daddy but my mother is screaming. We are "dirty rotten spoiled brats" and if it weren't for us she would have a husband that was not working all the time, fighting off death just to put food in our ungrateful mouths. I am a praying mantis stilled by terror.

I jump into my daddy's heart but it is no comfort. He is being ground up and spat out onto a Chicago back alley by a meat-processing machine, into which a gang of ornery boys has chased him. My daddy's thumb has been ground in half. His Russian immigrant parents are covering their ears not wanting to hear how expensive it is going to be to fix my daddy's gangrene infected stub.

"If he dies so be it. It's in God's hands," his mother tells the doctor. None of my closets stuffed full with winter coats he buys me every Hanukah will ever warm me enough to pull the frost out of his knowing that his mom was prepared to let him die. I can't free myself from his dying heart. Fragments of his gangrene thumb are inside me. I ask Horowitz if I can use his bathroom but I cannot vomit out all of my daddy's sickness. Horowitz cracks his window to clear out the putrid stench from his suite. I don't care if we smell up the whole skyscraper. My daddy is the only one who smiles for my survival.

Each summer he takes me away from my mother, who we secretly nickname "the mad vacuum cleaner" in his Buick. It's our stallion cantering across the land of a thousand lakes and forests. He enchants me with stories of how my great grandfather was forest-keeper to the last Russian Czar and how my mother's grandfather was a real slave trader in Africa. I am going to be the next to top his marquee from our long line of famous people. He asks me to perform for his department store matrons who wait for him all week to fawn over sweet rolls and coffee, their dowager humps pulsing as he serves up his chmataz spiced with corny jokes. The spinsters of Muskegon, Minneapolis and Detroit pay our bills. We never tire of him leaning forward and confessing "You know, I've been in woman's dresses for twenty-five years."

They will never ask him to come out from behind his vaudeville curtain and, neither will I.

My daddy and I are laying on the lounge chairs in our back yard whispering so that my mother won't hear us. I want his bedtime story to sooth me to sleep. Pretending it's a nice story I snuggle down as he recounts how my mother ensnared him into marrying her.

Horowitz lets out a snore. He wakes with a snort as I describe someone coming into my bedroom. He untucks my Dale Evans comforter plowing his eyes into me, directing me to watch as he unbuttons his pants. I am eight, no nine, maybe ten, I don't know.

For the first time no writing, no tapping.

"Was it your father?" Horowitz asks rousing me to beat the dust from memories abandoned carpets, but I can't see who it is. He is my fire dragon. The groaner stirs dissolving my quest for clarity, eating up my chance for remembering with her insatiable lips. The room fills with heavy fog. My doctor is roused to full attention.

"How old are you?"

"Maybe ten. No more than ten" My doctor gurgles. He doesn't mean to. I don't think he knows he has. I spread my legs wide with recollection. Vaginal nerves fray and spark welcoming my fire dragon's lightning storm. I pine for his visits to break open my little girl pretense. I long for him to trace his hands along my Braille curves, hoping to flee with my fire dragon from my infant's world held blind of touch.

"Was it your father who molested you as a child?" The doctor is cooing, a mating dove nestled in deviant bliss as my intruder consummates his pleasure doing things to me and himself I am too young to figure. He empties the innocence of my infant need inverting my yearning, binding it to ancient perversion. He rubs himself all over me, consecrating my skin with his forbidden milk. I lay awake crying as the white fluid dries, turning me to mummified parchment.

"Was it your father who molested you at 10?" Horowitz pleads. But I cannot talk. I am disincarnate, floating above my remains. Sex re-seals the urn's lid that holds my heart in vaults of unbreakable timelessness. Monks with empty eyes encircle me. I try to focus against their drone but it becomes impossible. I need to tell Horowitz they are threatening to ruin our work together but I can't because my thoughts are drowned out by their chanting. When I do tell him he says none of it is real. I am hallucinating. He wants to give me lithium.

Regression Session Four.
Psychoanalysis with Horowitz continues.

I am sandwiched in-between Horowitz's disbelief in the supernatural, and the circle of hooded men. He insists I explore my sexual history for clues to my fire dragon's identity. I tell him it is too dangerous. He still threatens to prescribe lithium to stop my hallucinations. I am afraid he will re-commit me if I don't pull up the details of my adolescent sexuality. My pelvis fills with venom as gluttonous gouged eyes watch silently from timelessness. I lean on Horowitz's authority to navigate the terrain of my being.

I offer him my recollections of Earl. I am leaving the safety of my first sweet sixteen slumber party girlfriends. My thighs lock down releasing the memory of that night riding on the back of Earl's moonshined Harley giddy with danger. We sail along the mansioned streets of the newly moneyed, scarcely stopping before we slam into the old English wall of his family's home. I glide, holding his hand, up the plush snake carpet to the upstairs landing, thrilled to be in his magnificent estate with it's chessboard floor of white and mauve marble.

"Want something to drink?" He slurs, Brando-style, pouring while telling mumbled jokes, looking up through sultry almond eyes. I do not notice he is filling my chalice four times. I guzzle down each goblet of rum and coke stolen from his daddy's liquor cabinet. With the quatern completed the monks fill Horowitz's office with approving sighs. Earl is flirting with me. He is shy, like it's his first time trying to make a girl smile. I delight in the expectancy of our blushing cheeks, laughing to his sideshow. When the booze knocks me down, his wiry six-foot basketball player's body struts up to my dissolving face.

"I'll throw your ass out onto the front lawn and call the cops if you don't fuck me right now," he slurs.

I am crawling to vomit in the four sinked bathroom but, before my head hits the bowl, he drags me to his bed and takes off his shirt. He is sweating our bottle of scotch onto my poodle skirt and angora sweater. I cannot stop regurgitating onto his jeans. We wrestle. My screams echo back the non-reply of his family's complicity. All night long I fight Earl off, wiping his head, holding him like a baby in-between his impotent attempts to violate me. I tell him stories to pull out the little boy that is lost in the booze. He is too drunk to unzip his own fly.

Horowitz wants more. I tell him there were no real bad boys in Westland Park, only frauds like Earl, scrubbed as clean as their motorcycles. They hangout like vultures on dimly lit corners, peddling good looks for a back ally feel; they were harmless.

Horowitz is not satisfied, I know what he wants. It happened years after Earl, succeeding where he failed. I was on a batch of bad acid, in the apartment of two University of Chicago students. They told me to sleep it off in their back bedroom, then they sent in boy after boy. As I relive the gang rape I turn my head to glimpse a shadow of a man watching in approval from far away and then, he is gone.

Horowitz wants more blow-by-blow. But I have exhausted the details. There is noting left inside of me. I make up things trying to ignore the cloaked monks moaning with pleasure around us. (My Las Madrinas home is swirling with a virulent chaotic force of destructivity. I struggle to stay in 1964.)I give Horowitz a poem I remember from my journal:

Who comes for me to dismember my moments
Refusing me retrieval rights on my remains?
Who are you that leaves me here spinning, slapped onto
*   destiny's crash pad wheel of fortune.*
Whose bull's eye am I
On this dartboard gone bizerk?
You have come for me again and again to re-stake your
*   claim*
What more can I give you?
What is left to take?
Only eyes of ether
Unwilling to re-enter convulsing flesh.
Eyes stuck in the franticness of falling fright.

I pillage my crime scene hoping this will close the dimension leak that has let up the hooded ones. But it doesn't. The room is shaking. Their cold heavy breathing sends currents down my last hope for an adolescent healing. My chest fights a convulsion.

He says the acid erased the fine print of my gang-bang. He asks me to remember more of Earl. I struggle to steady my mind so that I can pull his memory back through the chaos of the sea of darkness that has filled my doctor's office. The hooded monks draw pleasure from the abomination against decency I am becoming.

38

It is early morning and my slumber party girlfriends are pounding on Earl's bedroom door. "Natalie, are you in there?" Laying in sweat and warm vomit they break down Earl's door, finding us in a hanging noose of soiled sheets. They believe his story, that he had me. His lie is all it takes. Word of our night together spread across Westland Park like manure fertilizing stagnant imaginations, held too long indoors by the summer's humidity.

I contract mononucleosis. My phone stops ringing. The groaner and the monks are chewing on the bones of my deformed sexuality. Horowitz says "thank you, that's all for now."

As I return to Las Madrinas her eyes will not let me rest. She has been here all along, with her eyes begging for me to release her memory. Those eyes I wrote about four decades ago in a poem, the eyes of Nefertiti, my eyes.

Chapter

7

Regression, Session Six

Horowitz won't let up. "Was it your father who molested you at 10?" I retreat to the back porch with my daddy. We give clouds names, ignoring my mother who is next to us, pulling the skin off chicken, using the raw edge of her knife like teeth. My brother intrudes wanting us to see him all dressed up to win the howdy-dowdy look-a-like television contest. He's holding up a tube of Colgate. On his face he has painted freckles and a big phony smile. His Jewish boy's neck is knotted up with a bucking bronco cowboy scarf. He should have won, he looks just like the wooden puppet with the stenciled on grin. What he does get is his face smashed into his potatoes by my infuriated father, Ralph is eating too slowly. My brother's face is blotched with tears of humiliation. He's not pretty like me. He's skinny and does everything at a pace that drives my parents wild. To get them off his back, he begins to run and doesn't stop until he makes it to the State Championships breaking every record.

"You and your father had a special bond? Your brother didn't have that with your father did he? A bond that was consummated at 10?" Horowitz insists.

Sheets of moisture sweep the soot sky. I fear I am like Chicago, an uncleanable congestion of clogged moments. Horowitz wants me to concentrate, to draw up more pain. I do as he asks.

It's the year of my attempted suicide. I tell him, "My mother has locked herself in the bathroom." Her sister phones from California, my grandfather, her father, has passed away suddenly, diabetes, heart failure. He is only 65.

"You're a whole bunch of nothing." My mother screams through the locked bathroom door. "I'll never love any of you the way I loved him. He is the only one I ever cared about." I do not remember how she got to her father's funeral only that for the first time I had the house to myself.

I phoned my first boyfriend Tony, to ask him to come by. We had spent the last six months parking by the old railroad tracks. I was excited to be alone with him for the first time indoors.

That night my father returned home unexpectedly. It was the only ocassion he ever came home like that, before the week-end. Ancient contracts tumbled up the channel of my burgeoning sexuality as my father slammed his bedroom door. I could hear him call out for me as his trousers hit the floor above our heads.

Horowitz is transfixed. I wonder if he has stopped breathing.

"When I entered my father's room he tells me he has come home because he has taken ill. He wants me to check on him. I do, but I won't stay in his room. It has an awful smell, like feces and urine were stuck to his bed sheets. It's so dark; I don't want to be in there with him alone.

"Have you been in there before, alone, in his bed?" Horowitz whispers.

"I don't know. He's just lying there. He won't say anything. I go downstairs and lay a sheet over my mother's fake satin coverlets so Anthony's pleasure won't stain her reupholstered cushions. We have a fight about it. He says I've changed. I never acted like I felt our sex was dirty before. I give myself to Anthony. My father's moans punctuate Anthony's sighs through the heater vent. I fight against currents of enormous hatred but I cannot outstroke this sudden rage or my father's demands.

I explode at Anthony, sure all he wants is to consummate his Saturday night. I'd rather rip his art scholarship right out from under his easy future. My loose cannon sex has found its war. I'm screaming, throwing him out of my house. I tell him he doesn't deserve to take his place in the world of men vivified by my lost heat. My sex and hatred have become one.

When my mother finally returns home she is dressed in an old mink from her fathers estate. My daddy runs to her side, crying, accusing me of neglect. I never emptied his bedpan. I left him in filth with no food. He's lying because he can't have his little girl anymore, because I am becoming a woman, because I am downstairs giving my body to another man. My daddy only likes little girls.

"Are you saying because he can no longer have you as he has many times before he turns against you? No?" Freud's man breaks in.

"No, No you are wrong." I sob. The downpour outside offers comradery to my tears that, I fear, will never stop. My daddy's rage conspired with an ancient hatred that took me again with it from that night. I lost Anthony. I was never with him again. It was the beginning of a flatness that took me to suicide.

"Your father was jealous of your first lover after him? Wasn't he?" my analyst interrupts, but I don't answer. The Chicago skyline explodes in claws of lightening. It hits the post outside Freud's ivory tower. We are sent into darkness. My mother and I are tearing at each other across my adolescence, storming bargain basements, pecking each other like two fighting cocks over the color of my prom shoes or the best price for a starter bra. We attack each other viciously filling twenty years with sour ammonia. Our warring emotional energy is the yeast to raise my daddy's stale bread. Our daily brawl is his staff of life. He is living off my destructive emotion. The hooded ones are pleased.

I am a wailing wall of revelation. "Daddy you sabotaged the music of my woman's spirit and lived off the energy released through my hatred. You thrived on it for two decades. My beauty was sacrificed to make this bouquet of mother-daughter blood misery. You have been the black ribbon holding us at each other's throats. Daddy, you are a coward, hiding behind your crucible of long suffering, making one or the other of your women unclean, too dirty to sit with you in temple, but not too dirty to be your lissome super." Hail beats the window of Horowitz's tower. "Mother and I are your foul mouths biting open sores for you to suck." I won't stop shouting at my father and mother from my doctor's couch.

"Where were you when the fire dragon came to my bed mother? Why did you do nothing? Why did you let let it happen until there could be no female soul left in me. What did all this serve?"

"Then he was your fire dragon, your father?" the doctor asks, jingling his keys on the edge of his seat.

Lit by the storms high voltage, I see my fire dragon filling me with his tongue. We are two touch-starved bodies clutched in the locked claws of my father.

"No, it was never him, never. My father didn't have the nerve to incest me himself. He sent all that energy into his crony, my uncle and sent him to my bed instead. My uncle, my fire dragon.

Horowitz stands.

"Daddy was it when they left you to die with gangrene that you turned crustacean hard? Oh daddy, instruments of destruction grew from your amputated little boy's thumb. Years of drudgery, schlepping your sacks of women's dresses who was left inside my Jewish santa?" I roll off Freud's couch and kneel in grief mourning the death of the dream of the good father. Horowitz doesn't make a peep.

"My daddy was a crustacean welding power from a realm of unacknowledged controlling energy. He held our lives with enormous hooks. We were all trapped. "Why did you let me turn into this frozen snow girl? I am mute, except for acts of hatred and violent hunger. Is this normal, never to thaw, to sleep all day, to lay limp, pining for suicide?"

A bottle of sleeping pills was my ticket to the madhouse. I lay on my doctor's couch imagining again swallowing my last bad taste, waking up incarcerated, a mad girl, too dangerous to own a toothbrush, a threat to society.

This has nothing to do with your father. Your uncle's choices where clearly his own, and perhaps no one knew. These things must remain separate if you are serious about getting well. You must separate fact from delusion. We have to look at all the facts Natalie. Did you ever scream, ever protested, ever tell anyone? Didn't you pine for his visits, enjoy the physical contact, everything you have revealed here from your early deprivation would indicate that. Well then, you must face your part. Wanting sex with your uncle, having sex with him is nothing to be ashamed of. It is perfectly normal. The envy to possess the male member is deeply held by the female. Men have a power that women desire for themselves. Freud called it penis envy, but no matter what the label, it is a fact of life. Psychoanalysis will help you learn to live with reality. You decide when it is time to accept your life without voices and visions. It is in your hands to stop fighting against what is. Isn't that what you want Natalie, to be free?"

Las Madrinas, Arizona, later that night

Adolescent hatred and perversion grip my adult mind. My reliving has released up to the surface of my awareness a hell of energy I feel I have been breeding since my birth. Why, I do not know.

Kneeling by the altar I built for meditation and centering, I pray. What I consider to be my incest and gang rape form only one story in a world riddled with daily horrors performed on thousands of children who have no voice to speak and to this very day no way

45

to escape. I promise to persist in retracing the thread of my personal experience until there is no place left for this generational darkness to hide.

Chapter

8

The Cabana at The Shambhala Lodge, two days later

I floated for the better part of two days on Shambhala's mandala shaped pool paddling my rented lanai feebly like a convalescing arthritic. The darkness of my past ran through my body, inflaming my joints into columns of unyielding stone. A waterfall carried my raft into a second lagoon, surrounded by hanging baskets of gardenias. I bathed in their exquisite fragrance. It took me back to life after Horowitz, to the 60's, to San Francisco, to the summer of love.

It took me years to leave Horowitz. I flew to San Francisco, missing the summer of love but still in time to be one of those who danced to the congas, saxophones, flutes and tambourines of the Haight-Ashbury's Hippie Hill. For a moment thousands awakened to the need for a massive change. Fresh idealism rode on a generation's innocence and sensuality with a raw redemptive female force. Called forth against the back-drop of the horrors of Viet Nam; hundreds of new paradigms wanted to wake us up, among them, the freedom of rock and roll, natural healing, uncloaking of the world's mystical traditions, environmental awareness, and humanistic psychology. Nestling in the vortex I felt the wave. It was a delicious seduction that longed to melt the world, an impressionistic vision to awaken our slumbering passion for life. California's wild flower fields swayed with skirts and tangerine poppies. The sixties exploded with primitive creative hope to disperse generations of rigidity. I was there, kissed on the street by strangers, given shelter in ornate communal mansions, asked to belly dance with enclaves of scarved women, offered the strength of organic grains and legumes prepared in kitchens painted with paisley shimmers for walls.

A shiver shook my lanai as I remembered deeper into that summer. After Horowitz I was a barge of self-annihilation washed up on the cosmic beach of California dreams, a gutted turkey with flowers in my hair, waiting to be stuffed. I joined the meadows of stoned, spaced out eyes, letting my skirts fly up beside my sweet sixties sisters. I lived in hypnotic pursuit of my next high not noticing the new carpetbagger's wagons as they encircled us.

I was just another drugged hippie girl exchanging bed partners in the name of cosmic liberation, laying on my back as the new medicine men declared themselves our new "enlightened leaders." I wondered what it would be like now if we had made a stand for what was really trying to emerge back then?

Before I could answer, a massive wedge of a man, dripping long silver hair and beard, rose like Neptune from the lagoon's depths. It could not be, but it was, Abe Levi, my primal papa from the seventies. After a Beatle sung his mentor's praises hordes of maimed souls made the pilgrimage to Levi's center for 'Scream Therapy' in search of the cure for neurosis. Committed to instant gratification I fell for it, believing I could scream my way out of the past. Levi had a waiting list a year long. When I interviewed in his colonial mansion in San Marcus he offered me a free internship to become one of his therapists and an opportunity to complete my master's degree. I refused to see that his therapy was no more than the screaming extension of Horowitz's no care psychiatry!

"Oh my God, is that really you?" I asked shrugging off the synchronicity that brought him to me. "What are you doing here?"

"Yogicar invited me. What are you doing here? I heard you dropped off the edge of the world, Raratonga or somewhere." He looked like a sly bear about to dip his snoot into an open pot of honey.

"No, just New Zealand. Yogicar?"

"Yes everyone knows Yogicar. He's the force behind Shambhala's Festival of Light. He's really big now. He's putting it all together left-brain cutting-edge science with eastern avant-garde mysticism. When I saw your name on the guest registry I had to laugh. I snitched and told Yogicar I knew you, Shambhala had a expatriate psychologist turned feminist liberator in its midst. He asked me why you were hiding out. He's waiting for you to surface." The old heb kicked to the pool's edge, his middle-aged belly jiggling with laughter.

My mind raced back to the last memory I had of Abe. He was injecting syringes into our backsides after exposing all his staff to a venereal disease by insisting we hold our weekly meeting in his hot tub. His wife had left him all alone for a week to travel by herself. Abe was never one for being with his own company, even if it meant endangering all of us and everything he had spent a life struggling to achieve.

As the wind came up bringing the first chill of night, adolescent hunger tore through my body.

"You're still sexy as ever Natalie. You know I almost left my wife for you." He lied. It threw me back to the night he asked me to accompany him on a trip to Sacramento. I was honored at first when he asked me to go with him on his speaking engagement. He was invited to present his perspective on his travels in China before a prestigious board of psychologists. At dusk my teacher let me know he had other plans for us.

49

Making love to Abe Levi was a spectator sport. He made no apology for the stonewall of a man he was.

"At least I'm honest, Natalie, getting into me is not an option." He pronounced, shattering my belief in scream therapy before his semen dried on my thigh.

Why was he acting so different now? He was almost passionate, rubbing my feet with his hairy hands. My eyes lost focus as my whole body fought against wanting him.

When he finally wrapped himself in his Zen beach Kimono and slipped away on his Peking platform thongs I laughed tearfully aching with what I had become. I wept until the stars made a canopy of luminosity in the deep blue velvet night. The sweet scent of the gardenia's hurt with what I no longer possessed, the sweetness men adored in the women they loved. I prayed to the night stars, "Where is my sweetness? What has become of the energy of my female spirit?"

A gust of jeering laughter slapped my lanai into a dizzying whirlpool just as a fog enclosed my senses. I struggled but could not steady myself to read the marquee that appeared banging before my inner eye.

Chapter

9

Lucid Dream floating in Shambhala's Pool later that night

The whirlpool spun pulling me deeper into a lucid dream. I was thrown out into a rundown city, not unlike Tijuana's red light district. A flood light strobbed the evening sky gathering a crowd that shoved me into an old cinema theater. Squinting in the dark I fumbled to a seat as the silver screen lit up with the word's "Coming Attractions." On the screen writhing deformed women twisted, smiling seductively. Their gyrations unleashed a mayhem of agitation. Someone should protest this depraved depiction of femininity. I was about to shout, and then suddenly, I was overcome with hunger. Searching the theater for a concession stand I came upon an old box-car diner with a rusted marquee that read "Welcome to the Ground Goddess Café."

Starved, I found myself inside, as a lanky Garbo-esk woman dressed in a black waitress's uniform and spiked heals slithered

51

from the kitchen. She spoke in a low raspy tone and lit a pungent cigar, blowing smoke rings that veiled her face.

"Don't you daaare serve him that," the waitress drawled.

"I'll serve up anything to anyone anytime I like bitch," a second waitress rebutted. I took an instant dislike to them both.

"I'm no waitress," the first waitress fired back at me before I had spoken.

"Your not?" I replied disdainfully.

"I'm the 'Wastress.' Don't you recognize me? I waste time, effort, and resources; don't you know who I am? Sure you haven't seen me in your mirror?" She leaned closer, laughing like a senile witch plotting to overthrow religion.

"No I don't." I retorted.

"This isn't your typical diner, sweetie. We serve up, well, a different sort of faire. Have you forgotten?" Up close her skin was a gelatinous substance that vibrated slowly, turning her image a sour brown. Her hair, Medusa-like, was tossed with fury, her face obscured in smoke.

"Do you serve any real food?"

"Same slop you get everywhere. Everyone serves up just what they've been dealt now, don't they? No more and no less. You found anything that went down smooth since you been born?" As she spoke, my past caught in a chunk of bitter discomfort at the back of my throat.

"We were waiting for a dish like you, darling. Time we put you on the menu," the 'Wastress' announced. She had an arm full of bracelets that banged against her bony wrist as she picked up an old rag, then read it like a newspaper.

"Gang banged as a teen. My, my, must a' been real tragic, but kind'a fun, wasn't it, Natalie? Kind'a got you ready for everything that came next, you know, made you ripe for your next big role, didn't it?"

"What role?" I questioned, indignant from her assault.

"Say, Natalie, congratulations! You got the part! You get to be the next female messiah of fucked up reality. Yeah, you can be the next know it all psychologist on daytime TV."

Then, she turned away from me and orated to her mutant kitchen staff. Her grimaces framed the window, piled high with slimy dishes.

"Bet she forgot all about the gangbang. Yeah now she's a hotshot psychologist. All those years of therapy then she goes and forgets she got banged."

"Why are you so cruel? Why are you doing this? What am I doing here?" I beseeched.

"Suppose you figure it all should be laid to rest with your past. What about their past, honey?" She said, pointing to the restaurant's female clientele who were nervously checking the time on their watches, while drinking coffee and smoking with down-turned faces.

"Here, I know we got something you'll enjoy," she said, handing me her menu. It read:

1. Blackened War Worms on Toast.
2. Children's victimization salad garnished with infant crudite.
3. Incest Cordon Bleu.
4. Forgetfulness Flambé.

"Can't you just see her served up as our next feature?" the 'Wastress' announced. The stooped shouldered women nodded in agreement then went back to their cigarettes and coffee.

"Oh sweetie, you having a rough day?" the 'Wastress' asked, picking something moving from her teeth. "Must be starved yourself by now, huh babe? Why don't you just settle yourself down and try out tonight's starter-Submarine Sadism?" From the bottom of the menu vibrating holographs of gloom, bad weather, accidents, and injuries shot up at me.

"Oh sorry, I guess you already know how to make all that by your lonesome," she chided as the Ground Goddess Café erupted into sidesplitting laughter.

"What loathsome force has sent me here to encounter this slop house?" I demanded, nauseated as she served soot off dishes inch thick in grime.

"I'd love to answer all your questions darling, but we're out of time. Sorry! You're going to have to wait with all the other women," she said turning to leave.

"I want to know why, when I am fighting for my soul, I am confronted with this grimy hole?"

"Oh, my, my, she doesn't like our place girls. Isn't that too bad, since she owns stock in it," she replied, pushing her hard-edged face into mine, forming herself into a funnel cloud of bitter rage that locked me to my barstool.

"Isn't it fun getting away with murder? You'll do well here," she said, smelling foul like a medieval battlefield. Her femininity stunk with corrosion like a chastity belt seized shut with bile. Just being next to her sucked the oxygen out of my lungs.

Men waiting for their meals on her barstools went into an uproar. As I ran to escape the 'Wastress' picked me up, took me into the kitchen, then slammed me into her deep freeze.

I was freezing next to shelves of vials labeled "Current DNA" waiting alongside plastic wrapped deformities of women hanging from meat hooks in icy rows. Looking into the test tubes their mouths began to move. Icy echoes crackled. "Too much pain, don't judge, had to mutate, didn't know it would be passed on. Couldn't take it, tortured; forgive us, too much pain. Female essence mutated."

Just then the 'Wastress' pulled me out and held me up for the whole bar to see. The "Ground Goddess" was knee deep in takers. It was standing room only, like some Vegas tits and ass bar where every man wants to kiss ass no matter where they come from. She dropped me, smiling, then spread her legs wide apart and grabbed for me again. Locked together with her, I spun like a tempest in the very same hellish energy I had been breeding all my life. Then she let me see her face. She was reptilian with a monstrous beak and bloodshot eyes that darted searching for her prey. Swooping down she dropped me to pluck up a helpless critter fleeing for its life. She hummed a lullaby to herself, as it wept, begging, and then mashed it with her mammoth jaw. She turned to hide her delight, but we could all see the scales on her neck rise with the pleasure of the kill.

Even her regulars tried to lower their eyes as she clenched her teeth. She taunted them with the little creatures dripping blood, insighting them to peck her bloodied beak, like starved baby vultures.

"What are they eating?" I screamed looking for a way to escape. I spotted the theater's exit doors and ran. As I fled I heard her roar, "I'll serve whatever sells. It doesn't matter to me what's inside so long as they eat it and keep coming back for more."

I kept running until I couldn't hear her anymore. Engulfed in smoke billowing from a burnt out streetlight, I braced myself for another assault. But, as I moved closer I saw the smoke was coming from the pipe of a white haired man. A gentleness emanated from him. He was wearing a finely tailored suit. His eyes were closed in contemplation, as I watched him with relief.

"Good evening Natalie." He said in a thick European accent opening his eyes. I recognized that voice. It was Carl Jung's! For him to appear I knew I had entered some realm of archetypal reality. But, all I wanted was to escape the 'Wastress.'

"Of course, if that is your decision," he said, "you can flee. There are those who would hope you might be ready to end this," he suggested.

"How? Have you seen her in there? She kills and feeds those poor creatures to her clients with no remorse."

"Yes, imagine that, no remorse. It's baffling really isn't it? It sends one deep inside to expand one's understanding of the shadow self. Perhaps something is missing from our understanding of the collective unconscious, itself. Other forces have come into play. You might reconsider your desire to escape the 'Wastress.' Hasn't your life been compromised by a predatory urge, the origin of which still eludes you?"

"Yes, but the 'Wastress' destroys with delight. She has no conscience. I agonize for what I have done. I am nothing like her. Do you know what she serves at the Ground Goddess?" I asked, still reeling from my encounter.

"What if I told you that the hope of peace and liberty is being stolen from the hidden depths of humanities collective unconscious mind? It troubles me deeply that the world is still in conflict, mirroring this inner entrapment. What if I showed you a soul," he said, holding out his hand that cupped a dancing blue ember "like a tiny flame, and told you it was every soul. Watch it closely as it plays out its' life, searching for the element that might lift it out of oppression. Hope my dear, human hope, that is what your 'Wastress' devours. Its' abomination is what she serves on her menu. Do you see Natalie? Look into my hand. Look now, as that tiny flame reaches for the energy, the direction to transcend, for that passion, that subtle shift in perception that blasts the barriers of our collective past into a new consciousness of human freedom. Search dear, in the crevices of your denial. Shemura may very well be one of those that hold the key. She has that combination of bravery and female emotional brilliance to penetrate what men would not face. Has she not suggested you might live through the emotional psychic energy layered within the shadow self? This goes against almost every impulse dear, but that is because of what has occurred within the unconscious energy fields themselves. It would be my recommendation that you confront the 'Wastress' somehow. Wouldn't you agree Natalie?"

I could not take in Jung's logic. I was too livid.

"That's what she serves at the "Ground Goddess?" Humanities hope?" I shouted back at him. "She is the nemesis of all womankind; a woman that lives off the hope of humanity? I could forgive her as a psychic possession, a reflection of the cruelty of women who lash out after unbearable pain and suffering. But she has no remorse! No feeling! Women are the nurturers of hope, our bodies protect the womb of creation. We are the guardians of hope. We ensure the future with our love."

I was ranting to myself. I looked up and down the vacant street. The kindly white haired father of spiritual psychology was gone.

When I swung the door open to the "Ground Goddess" she was sitting on the counter. Her ugliness shamed my gender and I resolved to tell her so.

"Misery meatloaf, darling want to try some?" she moaned. "It's the misery I love." Her tongue turned in a slow circular motion revealing Jung's quivering tiny flame. The Café shook while she threw her customers flame after tiny flame licking her lips and repeating, "It's the misery I love."

I grabbed her by the wrist and made her look me in the eye. "I didn't know anything so vile could call itself woman." I told her erupting with some deeper personal vision. "You devour everything in us that seeks higher ground. You have a sewer for a womb. You waste inspiration. You waste children's minds siphoning their inventiveness to vision a true alternative. You rob joy and whimsy and gentility. You leave people stripped without the immunity to shield themselves from hardship and retain their wildness. You birth complacency, mediocrity pettiness, mundanity, routine. You drown away human passion. You have left us a herd of exhausted robots, a cowering lethargic mass too stressed to awaken. When beauty blooms you are there bearing your teeth. Before we know it you turn our reality into an orgy of perversion." I was ready to do anything to stop the murderess when I saw wagon trains of warn down souls trudging across the centuries burdened with war, famine, economic hardship, disease and oppression inside her flesh. I could do nothing to her as she sucked the light from their prayers. Opening my eyes I gasped with relief to feel my body floating peacefully under the Arizona night sky. She was no where in sight. I prayed I was free of her, taking in the universes of stars. I drifted until dawn, dreaming I was rid of her.

Chapter

10

Fighting against the vision of the 'Wastress' I returned to my room. I tried to calm myself with a mug of Las Madrinas dark roast coffee, but nothing helped. By five I had convinced myself there was no she-devil ingesting humanities essential hope living through me. After all I told myself, nothing could manipulate the chain of abuse I had endured into such a hideous end. The desert's restless wind tore open my shutters sending my body into fits of shaking convulsions. Unable to stop my frenzy I broke open trunk after trunk of my writings spilling their volumes onto the floor. At the bottom of one lay the latest draft of my novel, The Whores of Synchronicity. I hungered for Ocelay, the book's heroine, modeled after Shemura, with the desperation of a shipwrecked captain. I would ignore the 'Wastress' gnawing by bathing myself in the white goddess foam only Shemura could provide.

I read all morning, distilling the light from words I had written years ago at a time when I worked alongside Shemura witnessing daily miracles of healing. As the gray clouds baked to gold flying toward the sun I realized my writing described a woman's magic, a magic I could only capture with words. How would a dark harbor like myself ever open to the sea of feminine nurturing that flowed so generously from Shemura? A riotous thumping interrupted my pondering. As I opened my hotel room door two creatures, whose sex at first dissolved behind their robes of celibate orange, apologized while knocking Chapter Six out of my hands. Its pages flew down the hall. "We're sooo sorry. We thought this was Theresa's room."

"Room 465? Theresa?" I scoffed, put out by the interruption.

They gathered up my scattered text, like choir boys caught stealing wafers from catechism. Handing them back, in no hurry to continue their search for Theresa, one asked, "Who is Elle? How did she end up in a sweat lodge with a witch?" The child had bloodhound quick eyes. I was both irritated, and taken, with their entrance into my life. They starred at me with hypnotized eyes of obedience. I wanted to strangle their complacency.

"Do you really want to know?" I asked curtly. They stole a glance between themselves and whispered, "Yes."

A desire to break their spell drew out my candor. What better way to evoke Shemura than through reading them the saga of Ocelay?

"Why is your book called The Whores of Synchronicity?", the redheaded child inquired, as I lead them inside.

The words, "Are not all woman whores until we stop giving ourselves to those that betray the sanctity of life?" leapt from my mouth without a thought. Sitting back on my futon their draped robes loosened to reveal the shy breasts of two sweet young women.

I continued to speak. "It is a brave journey to live by our own self-definition. The world is set up in such a way that our energies are used and compromised; taken from us in insidious ways if we let them." When I finished pontificating, I watched an unclaimed sadness float above their dutiful heads. "Would you like to hear this chapter read aloud?" I asked.

"Oh yes, please," they responded in unison.

"It is volatile and could upset you. I don't want to hurl you into turmoil without warning," I added.

"We live in turmoil without warning. I guess that's the world we inherited," the girl who introduced herself as Charlotte exclaimed. "Yogicar says the world is an illusion, a veil of tears. He's so incredible. He mediates for hours every day. I can't be quiet for twenty minutes without my mind chatter boxing. Whose Ocelay?"

"Ocelay is the town's healer. She is a great deal like a dear friend of mine, Shemura. Ocelay lives poor, on the outskirts of Roslyn, Washington, far away as that band of old boys could fling her without getting rid of her altogether. Her gift is matrilineal, passed down through her family's women. Her presence, just being with her, evokes a great light that vanquishes suffering. She has over the years helped many homeless children. They always manage to find her. Most of them are running from abuse, usually sexual. Are you sure you want to hear all this right now?" I asked, feeling both guilty and relieved.

"A lot of us are with Yogicar for the same reasons," Charlotte answered.

"Forgive me, I haven't even introduced myself. I am Natalie Stearn, ex-psychologist." I bowed before them, hoping my gesture would offset the terror and sense of loss hiding behind their smiling faces. "Can I offer you a cup of tea? In New Zealand, I learned the proper way to serve a tea in the true fashion of the commonwealth."

"Thank you, yes, please," Charlotte with the blue, blue eyes and deep, brown hair offered. "This is Janis," she said pointing to the second young woman with red wavy hair, bright green eyes and a mass of freckles. Janis' body was rolled thick with a bouncy protective coating that she masked cheerfully while Charlotte was pretzel thin echoing her friend's emptiness with anorexic bones.

"What is a psychologist doing writing about whores and witches?" Charlotte asked.

"Sometimes healing can only be found after abandoning everything learned through traditional means." I paused, feeling myself deplorable, a succubus pretending to teach young girls the lessons of healing.

Pardoning myself, I went out onto the veranda. The noon sun revealed an oasis hidden on the canyon's far-side. How could a land so long dead birth such verdant green? I wet my cracked lips, feeling the wasteland I had let myself become. I was this desert, unwilling to resist my urges to draw closer to the young lives caught inside my parched lair. After all, I rationalized that even the fallen have gifts to give. I watched them through the shutters in shadow awaiting my reading, kissing the edges of my gold-leaf teacups with chamomile-dewed lips.

After tea and scones, they climbed under my down comforter, clearly guilt-bound as though their beloved Yogicar might sniff them out. This freedom they were seeking was not in the rules. As I began to read, I wondered what my life would have been like if there had been an Ocelay in my adolescence, instead of a Horowitz. In the chapter I was about to read, Ocelay achieves what I attempted with Riley and failed, taking Elle through a psychotic break with love and psychic attunement.

"Is there something wrong?" Charlotte asked, as tears welled in my eyes for the boy whose life I squandered.

"Yes, but let's save that for another time," I said picking up the text and beginning to read.

The Whores of Synchronicity

Chapter Six

Witch, child and Afghan shivered, waiting for the crackling fire to permeate the sweat lodge with warmth. Ocelay kept this sacred place secret, hiding it between Roslyn's mine-shafts, ponderosas and pines. It was gifted to her by her Apache lover whom she silently thanked as she brought herself fully into the present by singing a Cajun lullaby, while the rain beat like a ghost dancer's drum. The animal-skin hut jostled on it's treed supports, threatening to fly away umbrella like if the storm got any worse.

Elle, fresh off the streets and a decade of incarceration locked up in Echo Glen, eastern Washington's prison for child criminal offenders, remained motionless. Only her eyes darted with laser nerves. She was a big, brown girl with cherub lips and cannon ball black eyes dressed in torn jeans, a thrift store jersey, army boots and a purse the size of a horse-feeder. Ocelay wet the street-child's lips, removing the soaked blanket she had dragged out to end her life in the high mountain glacial lake. She crowned the wild fray of the child's icy cold hair with her elegant hands while Souza her loyal afghan warmed the child's torn feet with the soft white fur of his ancient Tibetan lineage.

Elle lay frozen, fleeing memory with her desire for death. Contradictions stirred inner worlds to collide. The conflicted madness exploded demanding either she die or fight her way through with a passion for resurrection she had abdicated years ago. Ocelay smelled trouble. As the moon bore witness through the mirror of the electric night, lunar tears caste healing currents on the doeskin walls. With gentle rhythms the two were lulled into a light respite of sleep.

Ocelay was wakened with a sharp punch to her jaw bone as Elle's body shuddered, not unlike a full epileptic seizure. She angled her feline hourglass figure to cradle the girl, letting her long ruby hair fall like a warm shawl. Her hands held Elle's neck and tailbone, easing the release of the terrible wound that burst from inside the girl. Those famous hands were animated by the fierce desire to restore life. Grief erupted in moans from the bowels of the girl, making her sound like the animal she was.

Ocelay's hands became living chords, monitoring Elle's vital signs, sensors of loving attunement. If the town's folk had found these two they would have called in Doc Whittier to shut her up *with medication. Ocelay knew if healing were to come for the child she mustn't seek to control it or expect an easy resolution. She wouldn't start at nine nor be done by five. There would be no pay for overtime or any relief shift to spell her. Madness didn't intimidate Ocelay. Madness? Divinity? Who could separate those bed partners?*

The whole thing with papa, well tonight Ocelay's rocket ship hands were going to clear the passageway, so Elle could survive the pain she'd swallowed; him doing what he did to her all those years. It was like being towed from the backside of a run-a-way car, tearing off bits of her while her papa just kept right on driving, not even bothering to see he was stripping off her desire for life on the gravel of his greed. It went on that way for two full days and nights. Ocelay just keeping things moving through the raped youth, breaking up the emotional fabric that held her inside papa's macabre chamber. It is there she lived, her impoverished mind filled with instruments of death and torture. He had set up shop inside the girl's emotions, chaining her heart and asphyxiating her mind but he hadn't counted on running into Ocelay's lighthouse hands. Papa set to shredding the girl up before she could taste freedom but Ocelay wasn't having it.

"It's my fault, my fault, my fault," Elle screamed, while her mama squealed those same sorry ass words that set Elle to strangling her, incarcerating the girl for her teenage years.

"He ain't even your real papa, child. You got it all wrong. He ain't even your daddy," Mama mumbled, figuring she could wipe out five years of rape with three lousy sentences. She didn't want to see how her daughter had dragged her "imposter" papa's dick, like a child's backbreaking chore, across her life, corrupting her spirit.

He was still there riding her hard, whispering slop, "Come on now, sweetheart, you can make it hard. Can't ya now, sweet thing. Come on now, come on." Soon as she pushed him away he'd roll right back on her. Papa was pulling on her heavy, reining her in, unwilling to let her and a decade of free sliding penetration loose. He tore at her womb, letting up a twister of self-loathing.

"My fault, my fault, my fault" she screamed, beating herself with memories of mama's yellow cigarette stained hands crawling up thighs, pretending to comfort.

"My fault, my fault, my fault" the girl wailed. "Don't pay it no mind, child. He ain't even your papa" Elle heard her mama say, breaking the girl apart where she was supposed to be building a future. By daybreak she was growling like a rabid dog, her eyes albino red, "Take those damn things off me. Your killing me with your hands."

Ocelay dug her feet deep into the dirt floor, bracing against the pile of hatred and violence shooting through Elle's spine. She jerked, scratching, spitting and clawing but Ocelay wasn't giving up. She knew this wasn't what it seemed. The child was breaking up the scar tissue of cruelty. Elle's heart, now thoroughly broken, had finally withered in a prolonged death. Now her soul drew a union with Ocelay's catalytic passion for life.

Ocelay's long agile fingers listened, pulling up soul beauty through Elle's matted hair. They stroked away semen and blood's recollection, untangling the girl from the debris of toxic waste. Ocelay knew the territory. She'd gone through her own "enlightenment" locked away in a padded cell, back home in Louisiana. No one there understood what she was trying to do. No one stood tall by her side, through the real bad loneliness when her soul was burning up a past so rigid it didn't let in any air, any light. When the pain from the past grows the mind that tight-fisted, it's useless. It's got to topple. That's all there is to it. But before it gives, the prison of mortal isolation closes in and that's enough to turn a strong man into a vegetable. The child in Ocelay's sweat lodge was no exception. She was set to kill Ocelay for prolonging her suffering.

"It's your damn hands, your god damn hands are setting me on fire," Elle protested.

"There's only love in these hands, child. The burning is clearing this all out, once and for all. Folks would be jealous of you, getting rid of, in a few days, what they drag around for a whole lifetime."

As the rain and wind howled, fanning Elle's fiery dance of shakes and wails, Ocelay prayed for her freedom.

Then Elle quieted, entering the eye of her anguish, letting them both rest awhile; their woman's bravery protected by the night's storm. Candle wax rippled and dried in a lake by their intertwined feet. As the first birds of dawn chirruped their salutation to the rising sun, Elle pulled her toes from the hardened wax.

"I want to love. I need to know what love is." She asserted, joyful tears wetting the checks of Souza and Ocelay as the healing team awoke, searching the child's eyes with binoculars of care. They held steady like a captain's hand, navigating through iceberg filled waters. The white witch knew Elle had made it through.

"How did you do it Ocelay? I felt you inside me when I couldn't make it back, when I had no strength left you were there with the energy I needed. I swear it was you and those damned hands. You made yourself into my bridge, you lay down for me over and over again, your love stretching out inside me, until I walked back on my own."

"You wouldn't be here unless you did the walking. In the end, everyone walks back on their own. Congratulations Elle," Ocelay smiled putting fresh pine logs on the fire to warm the rocks.

Elle starred long and deep into her new friend's eyes. "You don't change like everyone else. Everyone I've ever known is at least two different people pretending the other one's not there. No one's ever stayed, no one's ever been like you, good all the way through " Elle was back. She wasn't safe from the sky that *threatened to blow up a fresh cloudburst, one that could easily take their flimsy hut down one of the Roslyn coalmines. She had no money and really nothing she could call a direction for her life, or even the next day for that matter. Everything she had blazed up under those hands. But it didn't matter. Something was glowing across the magic of hands and eyes reaching for life and it gave her a feeling so foreign, so mysterious, so strange, so something that she didn't have a name for it. Then it came to her, she was happy, happy just to be alive. She stopped, captive in the real momentum of her rebirth.*

"What happens to Elle after that? Does she really live brand new?" Janis asked, her face flushed with promise.

"Oh I guess, she goes on to learn Ocelay's love's secrets and become a stomping force for justice." I answered half present, clinging to Ocelay's nurturing aura.

"Does she learn how to love?" Charlotte asked, exposing a deep melancholy.

"Yes, yes" I said, growing impatient. "Ocelay isn't done with her yet. She teaches Elle how to love and become a real woman. She learns how to use her newborn gift to become a healer herself."

The two innocents under my quilt smiled like love starved dogs with their first full belly. Yogicar's acolytes begged me to go on.

"Love secrets? Can you read us from that part?" Charlotte pleaded.

"Why," I retorted. "Isn't Yogicar your gateway to the light?" I was infuriated. They would have done anything to hear one more paragraph, just to be in Ocelay's presence a moment longer. I could see it in their eyes. Pardoning myself for the lavatory, I shoved the door closed against the jealousy I suddenly felt for my own character. No, it was worse than that. I was jealous of Shemura! My chest burned with wanting, to be her, to be the healer with the steady love, cleaved to with trust and devotion. I couldn't stop myself. Thoughts flooded my mind. She would never be lonely. Obsessed, I could see her, surrounded by love, laughter, gourmet meals made by devoted friends, grandchildren, Christmas, cocooned in her family. She had been Ocelay to three generations of children. I couldn't stand the contrast. My daughter would have nothing to do with me. She was the sun's zenith, I her envious shadow. I wanted to steal her life, use it's energy like gauze to mask my emptiness. I panted, unable to regain composure. I knew the two girls were waiting for me to be their Ocelay, their Shemura, but how could I face them? How could I be the same person whose writing I had just read? I had knowledge, but not the means to temper the combativeness that now grabbed me, shocking me with its depths. I could not stop the conflicted feelings that exploded towards Shemura, the one person who had befriended me, sharing with me a world of love and female wisdom, travel and adventure; the woman who always encouraged me to dive deep, to find truth. I gasped at my image in the bathroom mirror. Nefertiti's coned headdress appeared wrapped in her rainbow braid then her mournful vacant eyes. Her head began to elongate as I tried to pull myself from my jealousy of Shemura a separation appeared in the glass. The elongated skull was not hers. Someone else was there with her! I caught a glimmer of a second crown and then it faded like a photo's negative.

"What do you want? Why are you here? What do you have to do with all this?" But as I shouted they both disappeared.

When I re-entered the sitting room I looked at the clock. I had been in there for a half an hour. The girls were gone. Only a note was left under a half-eaten scone, stained with lemon curd.

Thank you Doctor Stearn. We love Ocelay. We want to know more about her. How could she be good all the way through? Can we come again and hear more of her love secrets? We didn't want to disturb you but we are late for our Sat Sung with Yogicar. When can we come back? Do you have other chapters you would be willing the share?" E-mail us at festival of lightworkers.org but don't leave your name. Love Charlotte and Janis.

Other writings? Sobbing, I ran to my closet to spend the remainder of the day reading through my tears like an orphaned child refusing to let go of her dead mother. As the desert sun set, strobbing my pale suite with bold flirtatious purple and fireball orange light, I found the article. I had published it in a woman's magazine devoted to the restoration of the goddess. It leapt into my lap with unashamed self-possession. <u>Shemura and her Men</u> would be the tumbleweed-twins next selected reading!

Chapter

11

Dinner was at seven. The lavish dining hall was packed with a throng of orange robed neophytes gazing upon their star, Yogicar. His chest was covered in flowered garlands, his balding head wreathed in Hawaiian orchids. A rush of yearning coursed across hundreds of anonymous smiley faces. Yogicar moved through the crowd like a well-oiled politician shaking hands, kissing checks, his charisma easing the hollowness of his herd. Laughing, his mane of thinning gray hair shook forlornly off the sides of his immense head as he fained gaiety. He caste his authority out, eyes pretending enormous compassion, but I could see their spaced-out carelessness.

And then, like prodigal children, everyone was down on their knees, overcome with reverence singing praises to this man for his protection through the chaos of uncharted times. He read from the Bhagavad-Gita, then reminisced about abandoning his career for long hours of meditation, merging with the divine, seeking truth.

I spotted Janis and Charlotte sticking flowers onto a curtained shrine. When they caught sight of me they ducked under its drapery. Clearly their fling with Ocelay was not kosher.

Grabbing my plate of new age fodder I huddled down into a chair as a procession of brides and grooms shuffled up to their wizard of id. The children at my table informed me that this was the night Yogicar decreed to end their celibacy. Adamant for the last decade that sexuality took vital energy away from the pursuit of enlightenment, he had, in one night of passion changed his mantra. My spinach pasta drooled from the corner of my open mouth as they recounted their history with the great man. For ten years Yogicar enforced sexless service on his thousand aspirants. Then, one morning he reversed his stance, announcing he was going to take himself a bride. Now, his centurions of celibacy following his lead were about to exchange wedding vows.

Sneaking out, I mistakenly flung the remains of my grub into the donation plate; embarrassed like a bad girl I escaped to my room. I drew the bamboo shutters closed against the desert sun and meditated, trying to cleanse myself of Yogicar.

Hummingbirds blown by the last winds of daylight bruised their wings, vainly trying to pollinate the painted flowers stenciled on my latticed shutters.

When the angel doorbell chimed I was sure it was Janis and Charlotte sneaking out through the early evening crowd, coming back for the antidote to the nights grim festivities.

But I was mistaken. Before me, filling my doorway, smiley faced, in silk yogi pajamas, stood Yogicar. He bowed walking past me to sit cross-legged on my futon sofa. He stared through me, like he had known me from a distant land.

"Charlotte and Janis have told me so much about you and your friend Shemura. I understand she is a great enlightened one, a healer. How lovely you have come to Shambhala for Spring. What wonderful timing, a full month of celebration will do you good. I see sadness and much loss. It is time to shed the past. For us all." He said, his voice unsuccessfully camouflaging a cold pull in the air that hung above me like a sucking tongue.

"Charlotte and Janis, told you about me?"

"My women tell me everything"

"What did they say about me?"

"They said you wrote about a women of great light. I take an active interest in my girl's education."

"Your girls." I blared. "Yes, they are your girl's in ways I am repelled from even contemplating. What control you wield over their lives. Poor innocents hypnotized by your changing appetites, one-decade celibacy, the next marriage."

"I'm a psychologist for Christ sake," I wailed, trying to convince myself I wanted to stand against him. "I can see the trap you set. How clever, preying off children shamed into silence by a culture that reinforces unspoken abuse. You promise to keep them out of harms way while subterfuge rules. You're all they've got. If they go against you they end up with nothing. Those kids at my table were too scarred to listen to themselves. You teach them to candy-coat their identity, to surrender their individuality, just to keep membership in your society."

The man elicited an unclaimed rage.

"Yes, and what of your women? Why are they blank, no sparkle, no boldness, and no self-confidence? Why can't they think for themselves? How on earth are they going to discover divinity through the likes of you?"

"And will they discover their divine nature through you?" he asked, putting his hand on my head like a parent forgiving a willful child. "I knew Shemura when she was running her center back in the 70s, I respected her then but when I look into your heart, the heart of her devotee, I see only torment. There is no forgiveness, no self-love in you. How can she ask you to surface this darkness with no support? Where is your family to protect you through the purifying flame? Do not be so quick to judge me, Natalie. I would never let you do this to yourself. Come to me child. No healer makes another suffer so."

Off-balanced by his maneuver, I let him pull me into his arms. "Now you will see why my women are with me. Allow yourself to be healed with the light from your own divine higher self right now. I am a master of light, an archangel sent to guide you through the fire. My grace, and the grace of my guru, will burn your karma. I am one of the hierarchy of spiritual beings recognized by the most high. I know who I am Natalie. I trust myself explicitly. I have been given a power to draw many back from the depths. No one needs to be entrapped in the hell of their wrong-doing, that is why there are men like me. Whatever you think you have done that is so terribly evil, release it now and forever with the light of the ancient holy ones who are always by my side. You are the only one holding yourself back with your notion that you must live out this darkness. Haven't women suffered long enough?"

I protested, fighting my body wanting to go his way. "No, you are wrong." I responded. "We have never been allowed to live through the depths of the damage done to us. I've come here to pull this up by the roots. How can I rid myself of the cancer of woman's stolen divinity if I do not permeate the bowels of its origin?" I spoke with a wisdom that surprised me, clarifying my journey to myself in order to survive his assault. "The mutation of my female spirit will only be perpetuated if I let you hypnotize me before I have unmasked its conception. All the energy that has gone into suppressing woman's nature all these many millennium needs to surface and clear, otherwise it is still weighing us down. Shemura has always taught that woman's plight will not change until we reclaim ourselves from our core. Who set-off this bomb that splintered our psyches into thousands of displaced puzzle pieces? As long as we are fragmented from ourselves we are ineffective at fostering even the humanity in our own children. Look at them, now gunning each other down in the hallways of our schools. They are the testament of the damage left to be healed in their mothers. Self love? What greater love can I give myself than to reveal the unspeakable mutilation of my femine divine soul? Your promises of instant redemption rob woman of that full reclamation. We need our energy back."

Then he put his hand on my pubis releasing sensations that shot up my spine. Before I thought to stop him he was fondling my clitoris, whispering to me to let my energy flow, to concentrate only on the Christ-light and to burn up my past.

"Natalie, don't be ashamed of who you are, you have the energy to release yourself from all this negativity, right now, with the force of your commitment, your light and your sexuality. I am only a catalyst. When are you going to soften and let a man ignite in you the change you hunger for? You have known this would happen all along. I see where your soul is trapped. The queen with the coned headdress is not going to save you. She is an energetic sand trap. You're addicted to falling into the mire, love. It's time to let go, to say no. I am of the light, say it. Use the kundalini, use your own higher light to end this now."

In that moment he surrounded me with a tenderness, a promise of intimacy I had longed for all my life. He evoked my passion for Horowitz, for my father, for my first love Anthony, for every man I dreamed would save my life. Yogicar was a talented clairvoyant. He let himself inside my body and spirit, reading my mind, feeling my emotions with me as they ran through the patterns of lifetimes.

"Pull this from yourself. I see it. It's moving into your head, into the arthritis in your shoulder, deep into your intestines, these areas of chronic pain and inflammation you can heal right now. Feel the tentacles that shackle you to the past, what has commanded you through your father, your uncle, the false healers that have come before. Your starvation to be touched, loved, known, has left you vulnerable. Let the light that comes through me embrace you penetrate your deepest nature and let you be free. If you truly love yourself, Natalie, heal."

As he spoke, shame regret and self-hatred flooded me. I wept, realizing how little I cared for myself.

"Shemura means well but she is damaged, the same as you.

She has left you alone to wrestle with unendurable evil. Wake up child. You came to Shambhala for a reason. It is your destiny to be here with us. My children may seem modest, meek and tentative but they are children. I have to move slowly with them. You can do this quickly."

He encouraged my tears as he continued to massage me. I fell into a depth of kindness towards myself I had never felt. I was entranced, captivated by an experience I had never reached before, sensations of release caught me up in waves of blissful light that seemed to emanate from where he was touching me.

"I have never made anyone who comes to me feel ostracized or unwanted. I would never tell them to suffer through their darkness in utter aloneness," he went on.

The next moment all my pain disappeared. I was both quiet and moved, sexual and free in a way I had never felt before.

"This is self-love. The greatest love of all. The only love any of us can ever rely upon. Commit to that love, and you will no longer have to burrow down into this hell you believe you must live."

It took me a very long time to speak because so little in me wanted to end the intense, intimate beauty I was feeling.

"Get your hand out of my crotch right now," I finally mustered the strength to fire back. "I have not given you permission to be sexually intimate with me. This is abuse. I want you to leave. I will not whitewash this journey. The love in me is what evokes the darkness for conscious healing. If this is not self-love then I will have to live with my own self- deception. My love will return with the strength of my commitment. My nature has been stolen from me. It is a mystery no man steeped in power will ever allow any woman to retrieve without a battle. I cannot believe you support my redemption, why would you? My energy, restored, would expose your fraud to the world. It's easy to see who you are, just look at your girls. I want you to leave."

"Why is it that when women get this close to freedom they have to go back into all that male hating? I thought the feminine principle was one of love and forgiveness. You say we are the ones that wield planetary darkness, make war, perpetrate violence and brutality yet you are like stone when the door is open before you. What difference does it make if my hand is in your crotch? Is your energy being liberated? Are you such a prude, sixties sister?"

"Get out," was all I could say. My lips could scarcely form these words, so profound was the longing I felt to prolong his magic."

"If you wish it, so be it Natalie, so be it." He said like a benediction over a corpse as he removed his fingers from my sex. Then he unfolded his legs and let himself quietly out my door, whispering down the hall "What a waste, what a terrible waste."

After he left, I lay on the futon, feeling strangled by the coiled springs of energetic thread he had driven into my womb and up my spine. The thread continued to knot my heart, throat and inner sight, while I wept with desire for all he promised. He had said he was only a catalyst, a facilitator of my inner light and love, but he was in me and I knew I was in trouble. I prayed to release him completely, but it was a battle with a large unknown aspect of my intimate self that wanted to stay connected to him at any price. In the time I allowed him entrance into me he had woven himself into my energy field. I had let him in myself but knowing that did not make it easier to tear out those stitches. It was a hellish process that plummeted me into all the feelings of worthlessness and lovelessness he had boasted his presence would help me remove forever.

The moon's first light shown on my chest illuminating his vengeful archangel's sword thrust into my broken heart. While he was instructing me to love myself, he had inserted it in my compromised heart so that I could not find that love for myself without him. It was terribly confusing. I was dumbstruck. I had let him become my own inner voice, hitting the open nerves of my self-doubt. And with all my awareness and protesting, I had let him inside to manipulate me. He used a kind of hypnosis that feed an addiction spawned in the hollowness of my soul. I had given him a part of my sexual essence. In the moon's soft radiance, I cried, feeling the ancient autism of my unmanifest womanhood I could feel I shared with many other women; squelched, left uncontacted for so many eons. I was broadsided by him, never believing such a man existed. I was shocked that I was so easily manipulated through what I had never become. It was shocking, primitive, unresolved.

I wanted to scream and never stop, chase him down my hallway with lunatic eyes. I wished I had tossed his sandals at him yelling "and if those two hypnotized lost girls want to redeem their female erotic souls learning from Shemura, a real being of light it's none of your fucking business." But it would have only given him more psychic emotional fuel, more of what he hungered for.

Chapter

12

The next day I booked a bus ticket to ride deeper into the vortex. Hanging my head out the converted school bus window I let the desert breeze fan away Yogicar. Wanting the aphrodisiac of the earth's potency to rekindle my abandoned womanliness, I breathed in the high desert aromas of pine, sweet-grass and sage. The bus clanged to a halt by the side of a dirt road.

"Here's the path to the old ruins you was asking about." Miriam, the bus driver announced on my behalf.

"It's only a mile hike to 'em and another five back to Shambhala. I come round this way just after dark. I'm only gonna honk twice."

I was nervous with anticipation. The girls said the ruins were magic, with more potent vortex energy than Shambhala. This spot was a sacred Indian ritual site old as Stonehenge. I was fascinated. In these first days of Spring I was able to pass in comfort, traveling into the expansive canyon. Its record of time was encoded in ribbons of magnificent purple, pink, auburn and gold rock. By early summer this would be an inferno, the hike an impossibility, but today cooling cloud fingers painted the skies with whip cream strokes.

"Lost?" A young man appeared, like an apparition with a guitar and notebook papers falling out of a worn paper bag. Looking at me shyly, from behind horn-rimmed glasses, he was a mixture of fear and sumptuousness. Before I could defend myself he was staring straight into my frayed woman's heart.

"Are you fleeing the latest soul abuser, spiritual hypocrisy in general or just old Yogicar? he asked.

"How did you know that? Don't tell me you're another of Yogicar's refugees?" I joked, refusing to acknowledge his tender hold of me.

"Oh I tried him on for a while. I prefer to take my Sat Sung with the cobra, at least he's honest when he's threatening my life."

He put his hand on my shoulder. We stood transfixed, in the shadow of the towering pyramids, neither of us taking a breath, smiling like idiots. I struggled to deny the immediacy of my connection with this scraggly youth. Something in me didn't want to trust him. He rumbled with apology, alarm, and tortured affection. His full Mediterranean features, black curls and minstrel's body invited me to follow him.

"Do you live out here all by yourself?" I inquired.

"Yes, just over there," he pointed to an adobe house on the edge of the ancient site. The girls were right, it was spectacular. We could have been in Egypt if the three pyramids were not flattened at the top, more reminiscent of the Aztec temples of the Sun and Moon just outside Mexico City.

"What are you doing living here, all by yourself?"

"Waiting for you," he answered turning to face me as we arrived in a field of desert flowers and herbs between his home and the ruins. The scent of lemon and lavender eased the tension between us.

"I was just about to have my afternoon meditation and picnic, then walk up the pyramid. Would you like to join me?"

Before I could answer the wind whistled with sadness and tears were streaming down my face. He acknowledged them silently. Something had drawn me away from Shambhala, to him, and the clarity of this canyon, where we appeared to be the only humans.

"There were many Indian sacrifices here," he said, revealing the edges of a cratered sorrow. As he was speaking I had the distinct sensation that he was holding me up, keeping me buoyant for something momentous, outside the battles I was fighting.

Kneeling he went on "I come here every day, I guess their spirits keep me close so I can help them move on."

"How do you know that?"

"Because every time I try to leave something happens to make me stay. Last time it was a robbery. They stole all my money and my vehicle. How's that for a clear message? Can you imagine being robbed out here, in the only house for fifty miles? And, when I forget to pray for the spirits, the rattlers come. Last month I was bitten. Luckily I always carry a snake kit. Remember what Yahweh said about the serpents?"

"Yahweh? Wasn't he the god of the old testament?"

"Yes, but some people believe that Yahweh was an import, taken from Egypt, where monotheism began. Are you interested in the history of religion? Did you know almost every major bloodbath has been fought, each side dying with prayers to God on their lips? I am a rocking chair theologist," he joked boyishly.

"Ok, so what did Yahweh say to the serpents then?" I inquired. He continued looking into me, past every confused decision to hate I had made, straight into my soul. He held me tight, in his vision sometimes looking away, afraid to let me know the depths of his sensitivity.

"A few brave Israelites spoke against Yahweh. "Why do you bring us out of Egypt to die in the desert?" They asked. Then, do you know what their god did?"

"No," I answered, suddenly frightened that his unspoken

81

psychic tunnel into me might be a dark manipulation. I gulped, fearing he might be a skilled seducer, a younger version of Yogicar, targeting women seekers, like myself. A metaphysical 'Ted Bundy'. It was then I realized he hadn't even told me his name.

"Gary, oh sorry, my name is Gary," he answered without my asking him. "God sent his fiery serpents down upon the Israelites, their bite brought death to many. They came to Moses and were told that Yahweh would save them from these serpents."

"At what price?" I responded, stanced for a battle.

"Do not speak ill of the One Father God. Take a fiery serpent and raise it as a standard. Anyone who is bitten, who looks and believes in Yahweh will survive." He recited.

"And what about everyone else?" I asked, but he did not answer. He was staring at me sternly, like the fierce patriarchal god. He went on in what seemed to be a schizophrenic change of mood. "I sing the spirit's love songs," he said, taking his guitar off his shoulders. Looking remarkably like the artist they called 'Prince' he sang me his lyrics to Born on the Planet. It was no love song, but rather a tortured tale of spirits born, crash-landing into slaps and rude hospital neon glare.

"How could that possibly help trapped spirits?" I asked, irritated, already expecting better of him.

"Just a friendly reminder that it might not be so bad they get to pass on out of here." I did not like the chasm of melancholy that echoed in his voice. Changing pace again, he offered me a loaf of homemade dark bread filled with nuts and seeds. He tore off a chunk of goat's cheese, and handed it to me with his chattel of tart burgundy wine. It tasted of his love.

"Here please, fortify yourself, then we can climb that pyramid together. Would you like to do that?" So many emotions wove in the exchange between us I was captivated. We ate slowly talking of many things: art, the new age movement, and the vortex. He was concerned that a fog had come the day before I arrived, casting a somber mist on the usually glowing path of the vortex. But, he said it was not uncommon, that Yogicar, and many others would come seeking admittance into the sacred, they are never accepted. Their rejection castes a putrid smell over everything.

"Sometimes what they are doing here feels so sacrilegious I have to get out. Usually, in a few days the Earth, with the prayers of a few sincere pilgrims, restores her balance. The Goddess of Mystical Rejuvenation lives here," he said pointing to a spot deep in the earth between the three pyramids. "And here," humbly placing his hand on my heart. And I remembered Shemura's words, "You will meet people and it will be as though you have known them for lifetimes." This young man knew me and this spot in ways I was ignorant of. He enticed and repelled me.

"Ready?" he asked.

"Yes, I think so."

We walked up the pyramid, his hand in mine, until we could see the ring of pines that lined the upper canyon wall, like a wedding band of deep green that held this spot in a holy embrace. At first I did not here the rattle as it filled the canyon. Our eyes locked in a spinning dance of recognition. I lost my balance and fell backwards down the sharp incline. He ran but couldn't stop my fall. I twisted my ankle and before he had caught me, my back hit something sharp, sending an agonizing spasm of pain up my spine. I could barely lift my legs. He cradled me in his arms and carefully carried me back to his casita home.

I sobbed, as he wrapped me in blankets on his bed. He rustled through his bags of loose-leaf tea, then threw a handful of medicinal herbs into his blackened kettle. He forced me to drink the awful concoction, then pulled off my hiking shorts and injected me with something. My thoughts were breaking up like static.

Paranoia seized my mind. No one but the bus driver knew where I was. She would never look for me. I was going to have to stay with this scrappy youth who pushed up against me with a dangerous urgency.

"No one has ever looked into me like that before," he explained.

"You saw the last twenty years in my eyes and it sent you down the pyramid. It's too much pain for anyone, that's why I'm here alone."

"No, it wasn't that," I stammered slipping in and out of consciousness, trying to deny the telepathy between us was holding me to a solid world. The pain was so great I was not sure I would survive the night. I had to share what had brought me to Las Madrinas with him or it might be lost forever. In the hours that followed, I slide in and out of consciousness while I told him everything, the fire, Riley, Shemura's research, the 'Wastress' and where to find my manuscript. He more than listened; he relived it all as I spoke, entering my mind, promising whatever happened he would record it and put it with my other transcriptions. If this was to be my final chapter I wanted him to send it to Shemura to help others suffering from this dark affliction of time.

He agreed and then I vomited onto his floor, fell back and sank into his bed. He rose from the rocker. I was sure he was Yahweh coming to kill me, his hands raised up over his head with something in them. It was a towel! He told me then that I had fallen on the rattler I had heard echoing across the canyon. My fall broke its' life. It died shooting its' last thrust of venom into my spine. The injection my new friend had given me was an old Indian antidote. The combination of the poison and the antidote was sure to draw visions from my poisoned blood.

He folded the towel and put it gently to my fiery forehead, wiping my back soaked with blood and sweat. He gave me his leather belt to bite when the pain was too great. My consciousness faded past his skeleton cow heads that were nailed on crosses, Christ like, to the walls, down his snakeskins hanging off sharp cactus needles, through the stone floor. I growled as my face contorted, my tongue spun backwards nearly blocking my throat. My stomach hurt so badly I feared its wall had ulcerated with what I had allowed to devour my destiny. Mental Anthrax taunted my mind with oblivion and, at that very moment when I thought surely I would die, my spirit was pulled from my body and guided out to the canyon's floor, to draw strength and protection from the Earth. The Great Mother took me to her breast as the desert erupted in symphonies of light, bursting the dam that had entrapped my heart in darkness for thousands of years. I wept, dissolved back into the atoms of the Earth's birth. Her joy exploded in me and momentarily I became the rivers of her cascading generosity. Her love resuscitated me. I was one with her, the alpha and the omega of her delicious light geometry. I smelled the moisture in the sand with my eyes, kissed mankind's emergence with her as human evolution ran like nectar across my parched lips. I begged to stay a child, newborn, a sister to every other living thing.

"When you have given back what you have taken daughter then you will return," I heard Divine Mother whisper as her ecstasy drained from me.

"Please, please don't make me leave," I muttered. Then, I was returned to the solid world. Gary was coming towards me with a fresh towel, then he stood at the edge of the bed, his face dark and stern.

"Anyone who is bitten, who believes in Yahweh will survive. No, no," Gary shouted, refusing the darkness that threatened to engulf him. "She's got to see, she can move through now while the veil is lifted." He said as though he was breaking through to a light surrounding him.

"I don't know how I know anything but I believe what I hear when things come through this clear. Natalie, I am hearing that this is the gateway to reclaiming your original female essence but you are blocked at its entrance because of what you did to your own daughter. Mora? Is your daughter's name Mora?" He asked. I nodded my head in shocked agreement.

"Without facing what you did to her," he went on, "you cannot travel back in time as you must to the play that will let you discover your ties to Egypt. Is there a queen with haunting eyes?" he persisted.

"Yes, yes how could you know that? How?" I protested.

"I don't know, I can't say, only that she awaits. She holds the keys to your freedom. Now that you are wrenched from behind your defenses it is a blessed time for a sacred truthfulness." He went on. Exhausted I was unable to resist or continue to question how he knew anything. I closed my eyes and just as he had predicted, my daughter was there real as he, before my inner sight. She was running in some sort of marathon race, reaching out her hand to me for the baton. I knew with an unmistakable certainty that this baton would allow her life to heal in victory. She turned to me asking for it but, I didn't have it! I begged her not to go. My former feelings of missing her so terribly flooded back into my awareness. On her twelfth birthday she had left to live with Shemura's family up north. We never lived together again. I hadn't seen her for more than a few hours in years. Gary was right. As my denial broke I was filled with grief. I had pretended I felt our separation was for the best all these years, because we had fought so horribly, but I hadn't faced the loss of her never coming back. As my body lay in Gary's arms my spirit ran after my daughter.

Chapter

13

Visions of Mora. Recorded at Gary's Casita

Mora runs down a corridor of mirrors. She disappears before I can reach her, into its maze of reflecting glass. Back in the Casita Gary guards my body while recording my words. He wipes my brow, wet with fever and encourages me to look for where I have lost her.

The wind has found me in this corridor of reflection. I fight against its gusts for what seems endless corners, then in a tall cracked mirror I see my daughter open her bedroom door and walk inside. I hear Gary directing me to walk into the mirror.

"How do I do that, Gary?" I ask.

"There are no barriers to love, Natalie. Only what we have allowed to oppose it along the way."

The glass turns liquid. I swim through her bedroom door into her room that was so often bolted shut. I am longing to find her inside, but she has taken away her sweet jasmine fragrance, leaving me alone. Broken messages are all she has left for me; leaves to compost, codes made of discarded hair pins, deodorant cans half-emptied, Lee Press-On Nails, a broken karaoke machine, its mike, like a lost chord, humming through molded salad bowls. Kittens play upon her scarves and thrift store dress-ups. Here from her carpeted forest of grime she calls.

"Mama why am I out here on my own, an orphan at twelve? Where were your arm's, your tears? You let him take me again. You didn't even give him a fight. Mama fight for me now. Why don't you love me? Why don't you connect with me?"

"I wanted to love you, but I didn't feel free to do it. Who didn't I fight for you baby, who?" I call, collapsing unto her bed. But there is only silence. My daughter is not coming back. I am a vulture, perched on the barren tree I planted for her to nest within. Her tears have soaked to gray the white stuffed elephant I bought her the last Christmas we were together. I press it to my heart. I am the pallbearer of our desecrated love, never again to be blessed by her sweet child's regal forehead, nor to see the smile from her little girl's perfectly curved lips. Her hazel, almond eyes and ivory cheeks will never again bunch themselves into the duck billed platypus. I will never again press out their fullness getting to see her squawk, foolishly, like the whimsical bird. She has lost the precious intimacy of sharing her butterfly metamorphosis from child to woman cocooned within a barren nest with no love. Her nest crashes from our tree of life, rocking me down its roots below her bed. I pass through her discarded pink mango lipstick, her worn figure skate dreams and her chewing gummed tarot cards.

I am falling, traveling hard, hitting the obstacles I put in Mora's way. My brittle tones, my demands, my voice without comfort or mercy ring in my ears. I sit in our kitchen and eat from frozen plastic cartons, just as she did then. There are no fresh tastes to open her tender palate to life's flavors. I perform the duties of mothering, without real warmth, without any loving feeling. It dampens the fire meant to ignite her potential to love. I am her blackout, my daughter's cellular Y2K, the dimmer switch darkening her hearts desire to open and grow wise.

"Mama, follow the yellow brick road," I hear her say. I wind down the spiral of mirrors until I am at her birth.

"She is pounding on my cervix, suffocating, unable to be born, with the chord wrapped around her neck. For sixteen hours I am strangling her and she is driving me mad with pain. We are in a little maternity home on the edge of a glacial lake in Queenstown, New Zealand. There is no operating room, no way to do a caesarian.

"Mora," I call to her. "The doctor pulled you out finally with his metal forceps but you almost died. Then you screamed for a year. I blamed you but it was the energy I carried that drove you wild. Did you finally see me that Halloween when I dressed up as the West's Wicked Witch? You awoke in your antique pram screaming costumed in furs dressed for Halloween as this witches familiar . Did you meet me face to face that night hiding behind my green face paint frown, my splinters for eyebrows, my twisted pretzel-mouth, my smile of crenate? I let the 'Wastress' come for you, baby girl, reflected through the broken glass of your mama's loveless way's.

Mora's hands come in acknowledgment guiding me gently to another mirror. In it I see the last weeks we are together. Her long arms and pianist fingers are pulling the petals off daises as she struggles to read her future.

"You love me, you love me not." she sings crying, fleeing my somber erratic greasepaint moods to seek acceptance amongst packs of schoolyard chums. They taunt her swaying to the biorhythms of the cruelty of their jealousy.

"Mama," she pleads. "Rock me through their fickle friendships." But I do nothing. I leave her in constant uncertainty. I never fall in love with my little girl.

I complain about her dirty clothes and the crumbs that flour her carpet. My tone gnaws in repetition at her fresh emotional scabs. She escapes down the hall of mirrors trapped by malicious intent. There was no comfort here. Only the promise of more of the same, her childhood racked with pain, left behind, brainwashed by my assaults.

I push through my fever and try to peel back the steel bars I have helped her build to protect her heart.

"I see you now daughter. You needed a mama in love with you to show you the rapture your beauty could evoke. It was your birthright to hear truth softly spoken as a talisman to protect you across the desert caravan of woman's muffled story. I chewed you up with my insatiable appetite for destruction, turning away, teaching you nothing of how to navigate your emotional tides through the stolen potentials of your soul's wounded memory. You were a child acrobat, needing to balance your genius on the high wire of faith. I was to be your good council, there in time to stop your fall with the keys to withstand the world's negativity and still shape a profound and loving woman's future. Like my mother, I doted on my inflamed arthritic hands, my worries and fears, disregarding your fragile pick up stick reality. Thankfully Shemura and her family became a part of your life. They gave you love and truth when I fled my responsibility.

When the angry girl in apartment 264 beat you on her front steps, I froze. You came home with your bruised eye swollen shut but I would not lift my arms to comfort you. I blamed your poor judgement, shouting, "Couldn't you see that bitch was just in a lousy hostile mood? Why were you out there with her pulling in trouble?" I screamed at you, Mora, my only child, standing in front of me with a bulging black eye.

I have hit the asphalt now. I live in the aloneness into which I cast you.

My daughter is not coming back. I see her ahead, in the maze, and I chase after her, when the corridor suddenly ends. The marquee of the Ground Goddess Cafe clangs with the surge of wind I have brought with me. Mora has left me back-stage in the old theater house. I look out from behind the moth eaten curtain to see where she has gone when a woman's hand grabs mine and drags me onto a musty old stage. I growl as my face contorts and my tongue spins backwards. Mental Anthrax again taunts my mind with oblivion and I hear Mora say, "This is what he left inside of me. Mama I don't want to live with this anymore."

Crumpled over with pain and nausea I sit on the faded boards of the old theater. Lights comes up slowly on the bloodied feet of an old woman as she sits down on a broken throne. Our eyes lock in silent recognition as she plays pathetically with the pieces of a coned headdress. If it were not for the remnants of her crown I would never suspect I was in the presence of a legend.

"Hello Natalie," she murmurs through her nest of knots tangling her hair. So you did show up."

"Why do you say that?" I ask, as she paints the fragments of her headdress with her bloodied toes. Leaning intently toward me she smiles, giddy with challenge.

"How did history view goddess worship after me? Oh yes, 'Evil women incurred gods wrath with their orgies of idolatry to the fatted calf, now I remember." Her laughter shakes the old theater with acrid bellows then, dipping her finger into her own blood, she draws ancient symbols on her forehead.

"I need you Natalie, to be my scribe, to write my play," she says, hitting her breasts and flicking her tongue at me.

"Has it been you all along putting this idea of a play into my head?" I ask angered by her impoverished presence. "What answers could a wrinkled old queen too mad to bandage her own wounds have for me?"

"I am the mirror. You and I are one. We are the same Natalie. You are a part of my lineage, my being. Is that enough reason for you, doctor?" she glared, bearing her teeth.

"No," I screamed. "All this pain cannot just come down to a play written by an old hag in a dank grade B movie house." I grew sicker looking at her. She was everything I most dreaded I might become, a pathetic mad broken down old wasted soul, alone, ill, with nothing. No one cared enough about her to bandage her feet or comb her hair. I wanted to run for the exit, but she put her cold hand on my shoulder to stop me.

91

"Merciful mother of life take pity on my damnable soul! Help me to endure what I set in motion, a generation of enlightened women who refuse to face themselves. If you don't bear witness to my story you will force the next seven generations into its stinking mold. I pass the gauntlet to you, doctor of feminine psychology, madwomen to madwomen, we can dissolve the resin that binds mankind to his curse."

"Curse? What curse?"

"The curse that has let loose the obsession to run from what must be faced. It is necessary to stage one last drama."

"Whose curse is it?"

"A man loved for uniting a fragmented people into one heart. For a moment he was the whole worlds' intoxication."

"Can't we end this without another drama? Why didn't you help me end it when you first came into view, in my mirror? Why have you toyed with me, appearing then taking yourself away?"

"I had to wait until you were so impregnated with the energy holding his epidemic of power together, so mortally ill you might consider the project."

With her cold hand she escorts me to sit by her side. Then with a frightening laugh she hands me a yellowed folder. Her play is smashed inside with insects, old flowers, and tiny rings made for the fingers of little girls. She pulls a box of black veils from under her bed and throws them at my feet, then points to the character of the Veiled One.

"Her, play her" was all she said as the curtain rose.

Chapter

14

Stealing the Moon

The Play

Transcribed by Gary for Dr. Natalie Stearn

Scene 1

[Nefertiti sits under the golden solar disk of the Aten, symbol to her husband Akenhaten's One Father God. She is frozen in time, then, slowly her lips begin to quiver.]

Nefertiti: 'Live in Truth.' By these words History remembers us! [Turning to the audience] Did you know my bust sat on

Hitler's alter, side by side with his other objects of black magic? Even now your misguided archeologists search to glorify my remains under the City of the Kings. Fools, dredging the barren slopes of enlightenment. [She laughs wildly] You won't excavate spiritual dignity digging up my mummy! [With the scowl of madness] My husband and I have left you braying in our darkness, parentless.

[I, Natalie, enter as she has instructed me, in black as the 'Veiled One'.]

Natalie: We're together now queen as you asked. What am I supposed to see here?

Nefertiti: The cost. If the hours did not bite at my toes I would not suffer from this affliction. Who did you say you were?

Natalie: The one you sent for... to alter Egypt's tide.

Nefertiti: Let her drown. That is why she was given a river great as any on earth, to cleanse herself of us. Do you come to rob me of my invisibility? This is love's gesture? You are a fool; I live to wash away memory. Do not ask me to strike alarm with forbidden recollection.

Natalie: You asked me here. Mora brought me to you.

Nefertiti: Do not ask me to fight my way back through his thicket where he waits to ambush truth.

Natalie: I am here for truth.

Nefertiti: He will not let it happen. He owns my thoughts. He takes his strength in my emptiness. He waxes and wanes in the tides of my blood. My only escape is into pretense and forgetfulness.

Natalie: [Embracing the queen's head] If your memories can heal the morass between my daughter and me you are possessed by more than oblivion's hold.

[Nefertiti moans and sways as the stage darkens. On a scrim above us, seven stars explode in a flowering fireworks display; tantalizing the darkened theater with spectrums of dancing light.]

Nefertiti: If I could alter the future with the utterance of words I would sing the names of the stars: Meritanten, Ankhesenpaaten, Meritaten, Meketaten, Neferneferuaten, Neferneferure and Serepenre. My daughters, seven warriors of light, goddesses, bringers of ancient star wisdom, darlings trusted to my care. Female healers come to lift and cleanse a warring past. Volunteers from a world of ecstasy, seed bearers of divine love. I was trusted to be their guardian. Our time foretold when the one mind would yield with yearning, opening itself to light. Out of our Egypt Moses was to initiate a new world. Seven great souls came to prepare the way. Behold my Egypt! Receptive as a bride expanding her senses to receive her eternal mate. Her mind filled with celestial music, and the dialogue of the world's most enlightened genius, her heart inspired by the great mystical poets, her body massaged, scented with the essences of flowers from jungles where orchids grow wild caressed by tropical mist. Every precious detail to assure a fertile union with the light of all that is. This was my Egypt!

[She howls, trembles, then falls to her knees.]

Nefertiti: If I could alter the future with the utterance of words I would speak in fiery tongues to burn down their dream of Egypt! Look! It is his tiger let loose to terrorize tomorrow! [She stumbles backwards speaking in tongues, then slips and falls again.] I haven't the strength to face their eyes when I tear off this maggot shroud.

95

Mankind is content to keep his illusions separate from reality, so let him.

Natalie: How could a woman renowned for her spiritual strength and beauty have become this flustered ruin?

Nefertiti: Modern woman, how many lifetimes have you squandered overwhelmed by the hidden orchestration of your pain? Your naivete leaves you vulnerable as this mad queen. [Turning to the audience] You who hold us at your helm of hope take head. Egypt, the breadbasket in your starving man's kitchen, did not always stream with galaxies of light. For a moment, life entrusted us with birthing tomorrow's mind. Akenhaten, husband, Pharaoh of the Sun, beloved, how they longed for your enlightenment to sail them out of their sunken shipyard of discarded decency. Once the whole world applauded our jovial court, as you shattered tradition, letting your family surround you in court. [She drifts to her zenith] How they loved us! We were their emissaries of light, Egypt's divine nectar. Husband, childhood friend, no misconduct severed us from our Mother Nile then. She cleansed our pomegranate checks, baptizing our youth with liquid warmth. I learned the value of wakefulness watching you commune with the regal river cranes; holding court with our temple cats. Akenhaten were we ever these children, dancing on the mudflats, spraying speckles of the Nile's red clay onto our laughing faces?

Scene 2

[Nefertiti directs me downstage. As we walk, she sheds her madness, becoming the proud beautiful ruler she once was. Akenhaten is in his chambers, being dressed for a rare public audience. Nefertiti assists him as their servants struggle to make him appear stately. His nickname, 'the extraterrestrial king' is apt. He has a grotesque physique from an untreatable illness. His oversized oblong head, bulging belly and spindly legs wobble. More than once he losses his balance and falls. In his city of Amarna no expense has been spared. Gold and jeweled solar shields of the Aten are everywhere. Nefertiti is excited to be by his side as he is assisted into the royal hall. Musicians play tribute. She glows as her daughters enter from stage left. Mora walks in as one of them. I cry out with recognition, but Nefertiti scolds me with her eyes to keep quiet. Mora looks at me with sorrowful eyes, then takes her place as Neferneferuaten, one of their daughters.]

Nefertiti: [Her arms raised accepting rounds of deafening applause.] Akenhaten, listen as your people applaud our wonders! [Their daughters walk towards them, joining them, to sit at their feet.] Nile's hope chest lavishes us with these garlands of purest innocence, gentleness in ivory and satin, seven sacraments. Let us all sing, blessing to their flowered sisterhood. [Harps, flutes, and Egyptian drums play as they dance]

[The crowd chants, "live in truth, live in truth, live in truth" as Nefertiti raises her hands in the symbol of inner peace.]

Scholar: [pushing himself through the crowd] Priest of the mighty Aten how can you allow children into our formal audience?

Nefertiti: Please be patient with all those that seek new form. This transition heralds our beginning.

Akenhaten: I apologize dear friend. But each of my daughters carries an element from the 'One' necessary to complete the alchemy of enlightenment for us all.

Scholar: Enlightenment is not child's play, Pharaoh.

Akenhaten: I am a humble priest of the 'One' true God. These are his angels. Come let him uplift us in celebration. Our future is bathed in the Aten's holy light of self-realization. Enjoy his delight. Bring in the platters of sun-ripened wine and fruit. The 'One' draws us close as earth-bound man to touch divinity. We are freed, lifted from drudgery. [His mood sombers.] Forgive me, I cannot silence God. Luck has given me his lips. All spirit originates from one source. The days of redundant gods and goddesses has ended, and with them their secret initiations. He opens the temple doors.

Scholar: But priest, you oust traditions that have been with us thousands of years. Some whisper that we are cursed by your new God.

Akenhaten: Here comes a light to pale the sunset search for Osiris' scattered limbs. One source, one truth to unite our hearts in gold. He is eternities redeeming father. [He gestures to his guards to bring in another solar disk, this one surrounded by the images of his dancing daughters and places it before the crowd.] He makes obsolete our need to rummage for lost limbs, we are mended. No more priests hidden in the closets of elitism asking us to believe in dead stories preserved in stone, no more able to help us withstand the changing winds of death and disease than sand. Here comes immoralities God.

Philosopher: You have imposed your One God on us everywhere. He is in our schools, our markets place, even our homes. You strip us of what we hold most dear.

Nefertiti: Beloved ones please set aside your former disappointments and allow my husband to be heard. Allow your mind a new bliss. Egyptians everywhere are meant to live in heaven. The Aten has come here inside, [she points to her heart] to still the swagger of your brain's fickle snake with the singularity of universal light. He extends to us a peace, to save us from fear, from the seduction of illusion. Let him be the spark to ignite your awakening. Akenhaten is only his priest, but his breath is spirit. Let him recessitate you with the new equality of enlightenment.

[The crowd cheers]

Akenhaten: [tears fill the pharaoh's eyes] We have our avenger, our justice. [He struggles to pull himself back to his audience] My mind is but his empty channel. You are the inheritor of his heavenly estate. I do not know why he makes me tomorrow's trumpet. I am only his translator. He allows this meager man to assume godly stance. I do not question his selection.

Philosopher: [ashamed to push a pharaoh so moved] I am confused. Where is this god of all the people when he speaks so exclusively to you?

Nefertiti: You misread my pharaoh. The one source, one mind, one God, is here within each of you this very moment. My husband is only the broken body God has humbled to be conduit to his harvest. Light comes through him for us all. The one God pulses at the very core of every living thing.

[From the back of the crowd a beautiful young man, Smenkhkare, pushes through chanting, 'live in truth, live in truth.' As the chant sweeps through the crowd, Akenhaten is carried back to his chambers, followed by his seven daughters. Nefertiti is left alone, her arms held high, washed in the sound of the chanting throng.

The Crowd: Live in Truth. Live in truth. Live in truth.

BLACKOUT

99

Scene 3

[Nefertiti leads me upstage. She becomes the aged mad queen muttering the names "Meritanten," and "your daughter, Neferneferuaten ." The two girls run downstage on a beach alongside Akenhaten. I gasp recognizing that Meritanten looks exactly like Shemura's daughter Taris as a child. Akenhaten is being carried on his royal chair. He smiles, then doubles over, racked with pain.]

Neferneferuaten [Mora]: What's wrong Papa? Come out of that old chair so we can splash you like we used to.

Meritanten [Taris]: Yes, please Papa, come with us. Mora and I have magic for you.

[The two daughters swim out into the Nile and, before the Pharoah can protest, they evoke the name of the goddess Mutt laughing singing and waving for him to keep his eyes upon them.}

Neferneferuaten: [pulling an urn doll from her skirt] Look Papa! My doll has the star's magic in her, watch us Papa. We can pull down magic from heaven.

[The two daughters sing, holding their dolls up to the sky. They are suddenly lifted out of the water to walk on its surface. Their father shocked, looks wounded as he watches them. His legs and stomach cramp with searing spasms.]

Meritanten: [gliding across the waves] See us Papa. We are magic. The star goddesses send down beams of light for us to dance on the water. [Akenhaten seethes] Don't be mad Papa. Here take our star doll. She'll help you walk on water too. It works Papa try it.

Akenhaten: [struggling against unending physical suffering.] Give

100

her to me. [He motions for her to give the doll up to him. His servants take it from the girl and hand it to the pharaoh. He breaks it open. Inside doll upon doll fall on the sand.]

Meritanten: [Her eyes well up with tears as he separates a half dozen dolls one lodged inside the womb of the other. The girls run ashore.] Papa, there is nothing left inside our doll's belly.

Akenhaten: That is because one night the moon came down and stole her baby and took her hostage up in the sky. Then she ate her. That is why the face in the moon smiles. She is well fed on your baby's insides.

Neferneferuaten: Don't be jealous Papa. You can hardly move anymore, and we can walk on water, but it's not her fault.

Akenhaten: Daughter I am the priest of all that is. My love for you is what ignites the magic of your soul. Never forget who we are to each other. Your magic comes from the "One Source", there is no other.

[Meritanten crying falls into the water]

Akenhaten: Come child. It isn't her fault. The moon knows no other way than to steal light from the sun for her survival.

Nerferneferuaten: No Papa! We talk to Hathor and Mutt, Neit and Sekhet all the time. It's fun. They have told Meritanten she's going to be a mama to glorify all mamas because she is so kind. They teach us when we are all alone. They fill us with starlight.

Meritanten: Papa it's true. They do talk to me at night. They have told me I have all women inside of me. I am here to help you balance God's new kingdom. They are helping me to remember that I have come many times before. They say this time I am to be rewarded for all my hard work, that I am worthy of an important mission, a mission like yours, to bring woman into your Aten's temple. Hathor tells me you are sad because you have forgotten how to play. I can help you Papa.

Akkenhaten: Silly girls, broken goddesses have no voice, no song no magic. You're magic comes from the Aten.

Nerferneruaten and Meritanten: [jumping into his lap, wetting him, and making him smile] You see Papa, we can make you happy.

BLACKOUT

Scene 4

[Queen Nefertiti has been sent for. She enters the new hall her husband has spent the last long months constructing.]

Akenhaten: What keeps you away all this day? Does not a Pharaoh's desire take precedence over the contrivance of a woman's day? [His words slur as his robe opens revealing his naked belly stained with wine.}

Nefertiti: Husband, how long have you been taking port alone in this empty room?

Akenhaten: Do not call me husband, I am married to God alone. Women are as dependable as stray cats. Were you able to hold your mind steady long enough to perceive the 'One' directly, you would not keep his servant waiting all day without one word.

Nefertiti: You wound me pharaoh. What sweeps your hall

with this chill? I cannot warm my hands in your raging fire even as it sends sweat streaming down your robe. What spirit cools me so?

Akenhaten: Egypt's greatest mind imprisoned in this body like some pregnant spider. This is what I must endure? Pain my loyalist servant! Soon I will not be able to stand nor see. I can now barely glimpse the symbols God sends me to alchemize this world. It is not he that does this. This bilious monstrosity I have become, no more pleasant to view than a pot bellied river toad, cannot be the pharaoh called to enlighten Egypt. Nature makes God's priest unbelievable, paying for what he does not owe.

Nefertiti: Akenhaten. You declared yourself the living light at ten. Do you forget your spoiled flesh is the gift you offer up? Draw on your one God's light to heal this obsession with incapacity. Have you forgotten you still have your people's sympathy? Your affliction mirrors their suffering.

Akenhaten: This ringing in my ears, will it never stop? [He prays falling to his knees before her.] Father, take me in the crash of chariots, I do not care how I return to you, but draw me back from the blood of these greedy mares who run me over with their hooves. Come for me father, restore me to manly stance. Part me from the company of nature's oppressors, of deformity, gossip and tearful sighs. Step out of my path women, you lunatics of the night, who have given birth to this minced flesh, harlots burrowing me down. I will save mankind from your influence. God give me speed to outrun woman's magic. Bind me with your force to unwed myself from her canker sore road. Let me rid the world of her rituals of bouncing flesh. Let your brightness scorch her inferiority from my racked spine. Fill me with your intent and I shall cleanse the world of her. We shall reform more than religion. We shall reform the substance in which men draw breath. Queen, it is time responsible action was taken. Our daughters still worship the goddess of your childhood's temple. You presume God's favor while allowing them to mock me? You, Nefertiti, who cannot gift his hierophant with even one male heir dreams to be given the force of immortality by using woman's cheap magic? It is weak, made with the carcasses of dead animals, stolen from the sun's light. Do not humiliate yourself by my side plagiarizing God's wisdom.

[He drinks from an almost empty sheep skin catchall of port]

Akenhaten: If he graces you with anything it will be writing my history, and then only because I have made you apart of God's legacy. As he gives me voice, you speak. Do not let confusion pollute you. Woman, you are the imposter of spirituality. My God has directed me to strip you of your priestess pretence, naked no more, whoring yourselves in your goddess's name. A whore is a whore. Your sex is no longer sacred save through me and the men that follow the father. We have been given the authority to expose you for what you are.

Nefertiti: [Her mind racing back to the nights she conceived her daughters.] You are medium to your port king. It has reddened your tongue with these injurious tones. Do not cause pain in she who loved you above all else, even as a child. You alone knew my child's heart, left in palaces to cry myself to sleep. You asked the guards to bring the coconut tincture that chased away my nightmares, a woman's potion king. The wine is villain here. Come, look into your lover's eyes. Do not condemn she that brings you life. You know your God has married us together to sweep Egypt into this New Age.

[Before Nefertiti can finish, Akenhaten throws his chalice at her outlining her breasts in bloodstained liquor.]

Akenhaten: Look on this, my damnable body, a woman's handiwork, woven from damaged thread, a throwaway piece. Through woman's womb my hideous form has swept into this world.

Here I shall enlighten her to the value of making her design more wisely. From now on this shall be your woman's temple. {He slaps the side of the obsidian slate as a mattress is laid upon it.} Do you know how many men have died retrieving this obsidian slab from the caves?

Nefertiti: How can you blame woman for what you yourself have chosen to purify your own light?

[She moves closer, hoping to soften his mood beckoning her maidservant to remove the layers of her gowns, her coned headdress, the jeweled bracelets, and the amulet necklace. Akenhaten's eyes are veiled in a foggy mist.]

Nefertiti: I have been your loyal wife. Can't I find a way to lighten your mood? Let me bring you pleasure to sooth this pain. You'll see, you'll turn, as you have done so many times before, bright and satisfied, happy to be a husband and father again.

[She kneels in prayer]

Nefertiti: May the new dawn bring us clarity. I place my gratitude upon your One God's alter. He has given us seven stars to chart our course home, brother soul. Galaxies of love showered us as we conceived each of our wonders. Don't you remember priest? Tonight we can conceive our eighth. Perhaps the boy you so want. You can again be the masterful one, preparing me to be the vessel for your seed. Do not let this chill seize me so beloved, my eyes loose focus. What is this thickness hung around the priest of the One God?

Akenhaten: {He tears off her clothes, dousing her with his wine. She stands naked and liquor soaked before him.} Woman, show your gratitude. You are redeemed from the stupidity to serve anchored flesh, the harlot of your goddesses' temple. You are raised up, now

105

you are his. It begins thus and will not end until each of our daughters is installed to eternal life.

Nefertiti: Our daughters? Why do you speak of them here in this new hall where you have made our bed?

Akenhaten: I did not see at first why I had to be born hideous in relentless pain. Now my God has told me.

Nefertiti: Do not let darkness consolidate in those eyes I have struggled long to follow, those eyes that have been my only haven. Please dear husband, do not say this bed has any place with our darlings. (She falls to his side.)

Akenhaten: It must be so. You who have born us no male to secure my God's inheritance have made it so. It is an honor to be bedded by a pharaoh. God proclaims me the way to his immortality. How can I deny this to our own offspring? Do not be selfish Nefertiti. You cannot have me alone. I belong to each of our girls, each must know God through me. Was this not how men sought divinity when women ruled?

Nefertiti: Not mother with son, never! This violates the basic tenets of humanity. It is not in the human heart for fathers to sex their own daughters. What will become of them and you? This will alter us all in ways I fear you have not contemplated.

Akenhaten: You are wrong. Four generations of pharaoh's have prepared me for this time. I have counseled with my priests. They agree this is the only way and it shall be so. Do not stand opposed to progress. There is nothing out of place here but jealousy.

Nefertiti: Do not do this to me husband. Please do not.

Akenhaten: Do this to you? It is already done.

Nefertiti: Egypt's pharaoh has never mouthed these drunkard's words. Let sleep erase this folly. Tomorrow we shall rule this land from God's sober heart.

[The pair fall asleep side-by-side. As the lights dim to dark, I am pulled back into the drama.]

Natalie: Rule from God's sober heart? This is all you say? The man must be stopped. Drunk or not he has told you what he intends to do. Stop the bastard. He's a madman. What keeps you by his side?

Nefertiti: Yes, that was all I said. You reflect me clearly in your sharp light. Pity you will let yourself lose it just when you need it most. Our mirror weeps with what we share Doctor.

Natalie: Then help me to stop it. Tell me how to avoid your mistakes. Show me how to be different. There must have been a reason you acted so unwisely.

Nefertiti: Thinking only of yourself? Wanting to save yourself from more pain? Let the play resume, psychologist.

Scene 5

[From behind a scrim the audience sees two figures moving together in shadow. Akenhaten's excited breath and a young girl's cries fill the theater. I watch as the mad Nefertiti covers her head.]

Akenhaten: Do not fear daughter. The tragedy of your woman's mood trapped mind ends with me tonight here on this altar of our love. It is not your fault you are weak. Take the One God into yourself, through me you shall dwell in his thoughts, and have immunity from suffering for all time. Your being shall be one with his. We have his eternal guarantee. Loved one you shall never know the pain your father bears.

[I wander the stage searching for Nefertiti but she is invisible to the action]

Akenhaten: Darling, here ends your struggle. Your woman's body unpredictable filled with wild, untamed desire is now a part of God. He alone can banish this evil that compromises your fate.

Natalie: Where are you Nefertiti? Akenhaten is putting his voice inside your daughter's womb? Don't you see he plans for it to overtake her own? How can you let him put your daughter's fate on his chopping block? He intends to incest them all. They will forget their chord to the divine was raped out of them. They won't recognize what they've lost. They'll be seduced out of their world of intuitive play into his world of mental manipulations. They'll be priestesses of his mad laws in place of their stolen feminine wisdom. Don't let him Steal the Moon, the very ground of sacred life, all that is pure being, true feeling, compassion.

[Six daughters enter. I look for Neferneferuaten but she is missing. Nefertiti has drifted, stage left, into her garden, where she uses her tools to gouge at her eyes. Before I can stop her they have swollen shut.]

Natalie: What have you done? Where is Neferneferuaten?

Nefertiti: I cannot see. My eyes are beaten, I see only darkness. Do not ask me to mend these lids.

Chorus of the Daughters: Mother, look, our father has taken

Meritanten, to his bed. Your husband impregnates your little girl to sustain his immortality with a son. It is, she who longed only to ring true with the exuberant shifts of nature, to grow in strength in order to birth the knowledge for us all to evolve within the laws of the Divine Mother. She carries the energy, and the energy to help men learn to live as one. Listen to her muffled pleas lost in fatalities fog as she suffers for her belief in her father's love.

[From stage right Akenhaten's ring of hooded priest-monks enter encircling Akenhaten and his daughter. They chant in low guttural tones.]

Chorus of Daughters: Here are his fleet of unholy men, advising our father how to live forever in the KA, spirit unbound from flesh. Four millennium of cowardly intent binds us to his dark magicians. His monks use their frequencies against us deforming the body of the goddess. Our incest violates the law of the human heart. They use Akenhaten's crime against us to separate them all from incarnate pain. We are the victims of their ritual of mutation. Here lies the underbelly of their worship. By incesting us they all achieve invincibility. With each act against our life Akenhaten separates himself from the feelings of the living. Our Father, you have let loose endless generations of politicians and soldiers, priests and fathers, all men who chose power model themselves in your hierophant's blueprint. They enlist armies to join them, without feeling, fervently committing acts of cruelty in the name of God for millennium. They follow your lead, with religious zeal, separating themselves from the Divine Mother's law believing themselves God inspired. They ride on the amnesia of your rituals, maiming those still sensitive to life. You have used our wombs to birth this atrocity in future minds. We came to cleanse the past of brutality, but now you use our potency to imprint future abuse into the collective mind, as a tool for power. After your reign holy men will sex children in the name of God. Men and women will hear your God's voice instructing them to violate their own children. But it will be your voice in their heads. This is your husband's legacy mother. It is yours to break his curse queen mother. Nefertiti, you hold the key.

Neferneferuaten {Mora}: [Walks onto the darkened stage] Your Egypt, Nefertiti, your bride. Look what has become of her. We are taken in your fall, wanderers, hiding, waiting for his curse of the mind to be broken.

Natalie: Mora wait. Tell me what to do. How can I help her break his curse?

[Only silence responds. I plead with the queen mother but she continues to beat her eyes in denial refusing to speak.]

Natalie: Mora please, Nefertiti holds the memory, but she is mad?

[My veil blows up as my body explodes with pain. I am being pulled back to the present feeling I am being torn apart.]

Chapter

15

As I regained consciousness in Gary's casita I could here the fireplace roar. My whole body ached and my head throbbed as I watched the cow skulls and snake skins turn into fiery shadows, making a light show on his walls. By late afternoon I was limp with exhaustion.

"Talk to me," Gary begged, wiping my face with a fresh cloth. "Don't be afraid, whatever was revealed, you have the strength to face it, to learn, to survive. You don't have to explain. I've transcribed it all here," he said pointing to my pocket tape recorder he must have taken from my backpack.

As he switched it on I heard myself speak every line just as I had lived it until the very last plea, "How can I break his curse when Nefertiti holds the memory and she is mad?"

"I said it all out loud? I can't believe this Gary." I protested against the undeniable recording.

Its true, its all true Natalie, its not really a play. Its a <u>replay</u> of reality. It actually happened just that way, in Egypt. Its just being relived in that form. I'm certain. "Take whatever time you need Natalie, are you having trouble accepting Queen Nefertiti?"

"What am I supposed to accept, that I am living some weird parallel existence with a mad Egyptian queen? That this crazy play is the only way Nefertiti can reach my mind? That my only child's estrangement is bound up with the lives of Akenhaten's daughters who lived millenniums ago? Why should I believe it? Would anyone else?" As I spoke my body grew tense and my mind began racing.

"It doesn't all fit together even if it is somehow true. Nefertiti wasn't the predator, Akenhaten played that role. And those hooded monks were…." As I ranted on it hit me, those monks were exactly the same as the ones that had haunted me throughout my childhood.

"They're here." Gary said sorrowfully, continuing our telepathy.

"What do you mean they're here? The monks? Where?" I fired back wishing he would back off.

"I hear them chanting from the pyramid. They came within the last month. They're a part of what drives me from the valley when the chaos becomes unbearable."

"How could that be?" I asked. No one else has ever seen them. They're not real to anyone but me, and Nefertiti's daughters."

"Real? What's real?" He muttered, entreating me to come out of my denial. But I wouldn't budge.

"And the Wastress, how does my supposed affiliation with Nefertiti lay me open to that hag living off humanities hope? They make a lovely pair. Maybe I should hook them up? What do you think? You're the expert in multidimensional communications. Have any ideas?"

"You know you're going to have to go back."

"No. I don't know that. I don't know anything. That's the only thing I am dead sure of. I'm exhausted, I can barely move, my head feels like a herd of elephants have tromped through my brain and besides who says I can? Maybe Nefertiti was purely venom induced. Can the Hopi's just walk back into their peyote visions anytime they want?"

"The door is opened." He said with an ethereal timber to his voice.

"I need more time." I shouted at him surprising myself, "How can I live with the implications of being connected to Nefertiti and Akenhaten? He was a monster and she did nothing to stop him."

"To change the future. Does that make any sense?" He asked.

"How does their hideous debauch change anything?"

"Well, I'm no expert but didn't you tell me that Shemura seemed to think revealing the plots of the past could clear the collective mind of their effect?"

A blind rage grabbed me. I would not listen to him.

"It was Akenhaten that incested their daughters, not Nefertiti, for god sake. Their pathetic tale does nothing to explain what has become of me. How could I have become this predator doing what I've done to Riley, and Shemura? Nefertiti didn't do anything, that was a terrible sin of omission, but she was no predator. How do you know this wasn't a toxic hallucination? Neither of us can know with certainty, can we? I may have pulled something up from the unconscious that should stay there, something that has nothing to do with me, really. It just wants me to think so. You know there are all kinds of spirits just waiting for some sucker to take them seriously. Come on, this isn't even my past life, it's some ones life that is over, done, gone."

"Do you really believe that? Don't you believe in the hundredth monkey theory, or the morphogenic field of consciousness? I thought that was at the core of your research with Shemura. Maybe you need to re-enter the play, see if you can do it straight, break his curse, see the extent of the damage done. It makes sense to me that a few strong stories fired into the collective at auspicious times could be replaying in anyone with similar character flaws. Isn't that what Greek tragedy is trying to say? It's just that, well your tragic heroine has asked you to kind of be her sidekick or something. It's not that big a stretch really." Gary suggested.

"No," I bellowed, "No more, you weren't there." Before I was conscious of my intent I was testing my legs strength to see if I could walk. The revelations and cognition of Egypt no longer interested me.

"I've got to get out of here. The girls are waiting for me. I need to prepare for their reading, I'm sorry."

"A reading? Of what?" he asked, wounded and bewildered.

"I'm reading to a couple of Yogicar's lost girls about a love goddess. It's a piece I wrote about Shemura, several years ago. Gary, think about it. If Akenhaten succeeded in carrying out his campaign against woman's divinity, how has Shemura survived to be a female master of love and enlightenment?"

"I don't know her well enough to answer that," he muttered shyly, fiddling with his overalls. I didn't stop moving until I had gathered up all my things, ignoring him as he withdrew behind his horn-rimmed glasses.

"Is it too late to catch the bus home to Shambhala?" I asked.

"No, you'll just make the last bus if you leave now. How fitting that you are staying in the Shambhala lodge, like Akenhaten's holy city of Amarna. Wasn't Shambhala alleged to be a sacred dimension of truth and beauty and love, where souls lived like they were in heaven?"

"Yes, how fitting, parallel farce! We both laughed until my stomach hurt so badly, I begged him to stop. He kissed my forehead as I began to walk toward the highway.

Hitting rocks along the desert trail, he kept up with me, his eyes furrowed with desire "Are you coming back?"

"I don't know, but, thank you. Thank you for taking care of me, you have been wonderful, really. Forgive me. I have to go now." Grateful I could walk on my own, I was intent on making that bus.

"Are you sure you'll be alright? Don't you want to stay for a cup of tea and see how you feel?" Are you sure you're fully recovered? You're welcome to spend the night." He bravely looked straight into me, but I disregarded his courage.

"Yes, Yes, I'm fine, I've just got to get out of here." I walked quickly all the way out to the road, without looking back.

ᴦᴦᴦᴦᴦᴦᴦᴦᴦᴦ

Miriam sat reading the local gazette, hiding her suspicious gaze beneath her Shambhala baseball cap. As we sped away, down the serpentine mountain highway, my cracked window broke the sagebrush landscape into two mirror images racing out of control.

Back at the lodge I pulled my parka up to my eyes and tiptoed to my room, grateful to be back. I opened my hotel room door to a swarm of gnats flying at me from a bowl of rotting fruit. I batted my way through them, opened the painted shutters, flopped down onto the wicker recliner and hit my voicemail. It was full of messages from Charlotte and Janis but I couldn't get myself to return their calls. Instead I spent the remainder of the early evening in the Hawaiian rock shower, lavishing myself in seaweed gel, while administering to my sore limbs. Then I wrapped myself in my familiar old terrycloth robe and sat sipping espresso looking at the canopy of desert stars until midnight.

When the angel doorbell chimed, I feared the betrayed goddesses from the stars had found me. I imagined them dragging me back to Nefertiti and her mad husband. I sat perfectly still hoping whoever it was would leave me in peace. When the gentle taps persisted, like field mice nibbling at my cupboard, I knew the tumbleweed twins had arrived.

"Hi, are we too late for the love goddess reading?" Janis inquired, her eyes pleading like a street beggars. I wondered, as I lead them into the living room, if Yogicar knew they were on the loose.

"Does he know you're here?" I asked, trying to be casual, while putting on the jug for tea.

"Oh yes, he said that the Divine Shakti life energy we receive from him is no different than what Ocelay or Shemura or you offer. It's all the same and we can learn from everybody." I tried to steady the tea trolley from quivering under my rage. As I poured the boiling water over the sage, they cuddled under my comforter. How sweet they looked, two rag dolls ready for their bedtime story. And then I was hit, like a drug addict hungering for her next fix, salivating as the steaming sage prepared the room for the entrance of Shemura into our lives. Unable to stop myself I took up my yellowed folder and began reading, <u>Shemura and Her Man</u>.

There is a love goddess in every woman. Men find her irresistible. The spiritual journey men must go on or deny is launched by making love to her. She is comfortable with her sexuality. She is the sumptuous sweetness that melts on the tongue of all she touches. She is confident with her allegiance to life. A profound playmate, a white swan.

As I read, I could feel Shemura's light forming a protective shield between the girls and the virile beast inside me that lusted to feast on the light of their innocence.

Shemura's mother died tragically when she was only five weeks old. The orphaned child slipped into a coma, and the doctors feared she would never recover, but she did and with extraordinary psychic abilities. Later, whenever she was with people, their unacknowledged thoughts and feelings penetrated directly into her body. As a child she had to find a way to bare this total openness in utter aloneness.

Her father blamed her for her mother's death. He abandoned her, sending her to live with his parents. The empty opulence of their Bel Air mansion was her only childhood companion until they bought a summerhouse by the Sea. Shemura found her first friend in the Ocean. The Sea befriended her and while no human came to end her aloneness, the Sea loved her and spoke to her in a language of pure being that she understood. Her cousins called her 'the mermaid' because she was only at home by her mother ocean. Shemura vowed to make every moment of her life an act equal to the love given to her by the Sea. She would overcome the tragedy of her mother's death and her father's emotional abandonment through her own spiritual commitment. She had become an evolutionary jump, lacking societies barriers of non-communication. The mermaid had become a human without walls.

Her presence conveyed a stunning force of female purity. She could apply herself to almost any creative act with genius and her psychic ability was staggering, allowing her to give a reading to anyone, anywhere in the world, living or dead, with brilliant insight and accuracy. When she grew to be a woman, a procession of passionate, gorgeous and talented men found her captivating. She elicited poetry, loyalty and unbridled commitment. Jealous onlookers accused her of casting spells.

Kenneth came to her as a consummate actor who aspired to share himself more completely with his audience, to hold nothing back.

Reflected back through her aquamarine eyes, lit like crystal candelabras, he would say, "It's like looking into the whole world. Everything that exists is there in your face." With Shemura, for the only time in his life his passion expanded to embrace forever. He could make love all night long without the desire to end in orgasm. Through her he achieved the openness he was seeking.

It was rumored she won such wondrous prizes because of her Marilyn Monroe body and Elizabeth Taylor eyes, but that was not what kept their devotion.

Hollywood's producers were befuddled when she walked away from their offer of stardom after telling her "We don't have to do anything to change you, you've got it all."

I put my head to my chest not wanting the girls to see my expression. A future of stardom? It was unthinkable! I would never have walked away.

"What did she do as a child?" Charlotte asked forcing me to return to my manuscript.

She would turn tree limbs and junk piled in her grandparent's garage into works of art. Staring for entire afternoons at great museum paintings, she would return home, sneak under her bed with pastels and sketch them all night from memory.

Instead of watching television she would talk to the stars or lay herself out on her grandparent's balcony for a moon bath. While her girlfriends honed the art of catching husbands, she fell in love with Latin and investigated the origins of religion and the practices of Salem's witch population.

When she married and became pregnant, her dear friend nicknamed Phillip Peanut Butter arrived to pay her his annual visit. He declared,

"You are like a Madonna! A Madonna looks terrible with a vacuum cleaner!" He asked to stay and do everything for her to nourish her through to the end of her pregnancy. If the road had lead Phillip to women it would have lead him to her. As it was he preferred men.

Her home in the Santa Cruz Mountains was lovingly referred to by a generation of explorers as the "Cosmic Garage."

From its tree house vista she seeded spiritual appetites with her original mix of sensuality and soul intelligence. She designed her home out of living things; hand carved wood, stain glass, rock and mosaic. Exotic flowers were arranged in hand blown glass vases next to arched doors opening out onto the stars. Twenty or thirty artists, cosmic gypsies and enlightened thinkers regularly lit their palettes with her gourmet cuisine layered in three or more distinct counterpoints of bursting spice. She would send them off in ripples of laughter with her sneezing fits forgetting she was allergic to Acacia. At her request, Phillip brought bundles inside so that her guests could feel "the happiness of the fields"

After diner they would stretch contentedly on her redwood

patio, ready to expand with the universe of stars. Her favorite Indian musicians, friends of Ravi Shankar, played their finest sitar, accompanied by the deep base of frogs and Merlin, her pet Owl's high pitched staccato. Then Phillip washed their hands in rose water.

He treasured the hours when, still with child, she lost herself to her edible sculptures. He said it was better than a psychedelic to be with her as she dissolved into Debussy, while finger-painting the frosting onto her rainbow desert cakes. He would prance, counterbalancing her escapades out to her spa where her guests bathed naked in a cathedral of Redwoods. She loved to be with her friends as they "shed their skins of deadness." Then as she watched Phillip wrapping them in hand batiked towels she would fall happily to sleep.

At sun up Phillip made sure her pregnant belly met the dawn in private reverie. He tiptoed with his lace apron barely covering his naked chest to close her loft's quilted curtain, his long blonde hair fanned like a peacocks as he pulled the cord. Waking slowly she chatted with Merlin. Sometimes Phillip would prepare eggs benedict, leaving her free to absorb the colors of the wildflower fields into her womb. Afterwards, privately, he would feed Merlin field mice saving her from the animal sacrifice.

It was a glorious bargain. In exchange for giving her peace and natural beauty to fortify her soon to be born daughter, Taris, Phillip could ride the high of Shemura's energy.

Suddenly, flushed, I turned away, seeing in my mind's eye Meritanten shift into Taris then return to her Egyptian form. I tried to pull myself back to the story. Could Shemura's daughter, Taris, really have been one of Nefertiti and Akenhaten's daughters in Egypt? Could she be living again, as the shy competent loyal beautiful daughter of Shemura today?

Shemura had a very difficult time raising her as a child. Was it partially because she was helping her heal from the damage Nefertiti and Akenhaten had wrecked upon her? I forced these questions out of my mind as Janis wined. "I don't understand. Can you describe how it really was with a man in Shemura's life?"

"Ah, so you do want to learn how to step outside the known, to win the admiration of men?" I joked, struggling to swallow my realization and the want for what was to come next.

Shemura's castle home, in the south of Spain, overlooked Gibraltar. It sat like a noble dream of past glory, tithed to the peasants and pigeons. Outside the fortressed walls, boulders were legend to roam the mountaintop at night, whispering the Earth's untold stories. Shemura listened as the echoing chants of the moors dueled the madrigals of Christendom and the wails of the Jews. She quieted their warring spirits. And, even though she chose the solitude of this remote setting, glorious men found their way to her door.

"I must talk with you," implored the Basque soldier, his black hair and blue green eyes with the sensuous longing of Elvis's.

"I have to be with you." He pleaded from inside the tiny, stone castle bar as Shemura sipped espresso, banishing gloom with a young aficionado strumming her favorite flamenco. Her blonde hair formed a shawl of gold across her creamy bare shoulders. He watched as the flamboyant white-haired poet, Juan Rico, preformed his poetry for her. The soldier hungered to be the bard's words, penetrating the mystery of her essence. Rising from the bar stool his black leather boots silenced even the drunks.

"Your soul is so beautiful," he sang out as the bar keeper, Andreas, poured another cerveza, scanning the campo for help!

But the soldier was not drunk, he only had a few beers.

She left Andreas' quietly taking Taris up the old Roman steps. Turning the key to her church house door she discovered him sitting on her bed.

"I must to be with you," he again declared.

Laurence, her present lover, alerted by Andreas, somehow got the soldier to leave. He was made to evacuate the region. A realm lost inside that soldier beckoned with such urgency he risked his whole future, without a thought, just to be near her. That's the force of a true love goddess!

Laurence and the soldier were two polarities ignited by her fire.

Laurence was a child prodigy. He waited six years, dreaming of the time when he could begin his odyssey to authenticity by becoming her lover. For Shemura, lovemaking is a way of learning about the soul, through the intimacy of selves. Manuals? Training? I do this to you, you do that to me. No, no, no! She would say, "One must pay the price to become a self, without a self there is no real feeling so what good is intimacy? But with it, aaahhh lovemaking becomes an act of spiritual discovery!"

I had struck an open nerve. Charlotte and Janis looked in bewilderment at one another as I scurried to soften the blow. "There is a love goddess in every woman." I countered. It worked. They lifted their gaze, hopefully allowing me to read on.

Lawrence drew her admiration with his love of literature. He desired to give her his total devotion. He was in need of a way to heal. His own mother had set him up with drugs at twelve years old then turned him over to the police. When they locked him up, she refused to even see him. He was taken to a reform school where 'sensitivity was a punishable offense.' This drove his hatred of his mother in even more deeply.

As the ice plants blossomed, heralding the triumph of spring, Shemura and Laurence became lovers, lying together on a cliff close to her beloved sea.

Life responded to their pure intent sweeping them into cascading rivers of fluid art. Their lovemaking became a union with all creation, the bliss of Nirvana, the oneness with what we call God. It was a symphonic sojourn from sonnet to ode, from fugue to flamenco, visiting worlds of transcendent expression. They entered the creative dimension from which sacred art is born, floating on the lotus ponds of Renoir, glistening with the dew from the verdant gardens of Monet, turning into sea nymphs playing to the water music of her beloved Debussy. Laurence learned to move slowly, her beauty enlivening every sense, until his passion unlocked her pleasure. Their orgasm was an act of purification, an ecstatic communion that thrust them both outside the pain and duality of all they had endured. Transformed! Two joyous beings filled with light.

Such tales of illumination are accepted in the Ashrams of the great Avatars, not from the boudoirs of women. But Laurence was only one of the treasured men who attained great truth through the pure sharing of their sexuality and emotions.

Krishanmurti, one of the world's most highly acclaimed spiritual teachers, instructed his students to question every thought and feeling in order to reach such exalted states. Shemura directly encountered the deepest motivations and drives within the men in front of her. Both of them believed man need not repeat the cycles of history and could achieve this goal through a new mind created out of a transmutation of light and love. The purity of both of these spiritual beings was brought to fruition by their vast commitments to an enlightened humanity. This is what makes them equals. She matched his light with her love to stand only within the truth she perceived directly from life, giving it expression as a woman. He taught the elimination of all outside influence for the self to be born in the pure stream of the present. Krishnamurti was renown throughout India, heralded by the theosophists as the next great, enlightened world master. But he refused the role. She refused to use her psychic gifts, dedicating herself to augmenting only the direct means to free mankind from hereditary cruelty through her brilliant work in emotional intelligence. He continued throughout his life to defy the definitions others thrust upon his reality. She made every moment a prayer to life; a gift embodying spiritual truth discovered through the sharing of the deep intuitive, mindful self, exchanged through sensuality, emotion and, with her intimate partners, sexual ecstasy.

Every man had to make his own choice to integrate or reject what he was given. Sadly after several years of impassioned bliss, Laurence let his hatred of his mother take him from their stream trapping him in a miasma. Hatred turned him into a boot soldier walking the muddied fields of man, caught up in the cycles of violence and abuse. Warring men pounded across the viscera of his cellular memory as his connection severed and he was left behind. Hatred for his mother drove him from her. It yanked him from their river back into the shared mind of men, then hurled him down the centuries of aggression. Far away, her eyes reflected him, steely cold.

She told him, "You must stop this hatred for your mother." But he would not listen. While Shemura held open the door, he sank into an amnesia, forgetting his longing to feel the sweetness of her gentle pulse rising molten under his touch. He lost the yearning to harmonize within the natural surges of their internal tides.

The love goddess who walked away from falseness had the ability to midwife her lovers back to life restoring their beauty and sacred connection but to achieve this spiritual renaissance they had to cleanse themselves of the deep shadow they carried.

I put my manuscript down as I felt my face knarl and my jaw contract.

"Not her, not for her, not for Shemura" I screamed in my mind. I could barely remain in the room. My eyes were losing focus. I was overcome with the desire to devour Shemura, to possess her beauty to ingest her light. I sat back overcome with self-loathing and bestial hunger.

This perverse yearning could not be mine, I told myself as I struggled not to show my upset to the children in my care.

I could, at the very least, remain civil, I told myself, for their sake. I pulled myself together certain they would have a slew of questions for me after <u>Shemura and Her Men.</u>

I forced myself to think of their welfare. What would happen now for them? How would they resolve the chasm between Yogicar and Shemura? Oddly neither of them spoke a word. As I stumbled towards the shutters to let in the last rays of moonlight I gasped. The picture I had put on the coffee table of Shemura was devoid of her energy. It had been a photo of her glowing tenderly her arms wrapped around her Spanish donkey. Her magic melded with the castles, its surrounding fields, and her beloved peasant family smiling beside her bathed in the aura of her love. But it was no longer the picture that I kept to inspire me with her love of life. She wasn't there, she looked old and haggard, drained of her spirit. When I turned to face Charlotte and Janis the two looked satisfied, like wolves after a kill. I fumbled to put on one of Shemura's favorite Indian ragas, then excused myself. Leaning up against the mirrored bathroom wall I sobbed. Was this thing I had become, being passed down generations of DNA as Jung, Shemura and Gary tried to warn me? Were these young woman becoming emotional psychic energy vampires? Was this truly the nature of my own deep shadow self? How could this be true?

As I asked these questions one of the glass tiles loosened from the top of the wall then fell hitting the top of my head. Glass was everywhere. I collapsed onto the floor. My last recollection was staring at my bloodied toes as she grabbed me and pulled me through the reflecting glass back into the madness of Egypt, back into a world I had done my very best to escape.

Chapter

16

Stealing the Moon

ACT II

Scene I

[Nefertiti guides me upstage to her broken throne. She sits me upon it then turns my head toward the action.]

Natalie: Why have you brought me back?
Nefertiti: She has slipped through my hands like desert sand. She is yours now. Careful, careful. You don't know the preciousness you hold.
Natalie: Mora? Taris? Who do I hold?
Nefertiti: There.

[She points to three of her daughters. Meritaten known as Mye, and Ankhesenpaaten, known as Nekeet are in the royal bathhouse massaging their eldest sister Setepenre known as Sheeh. They play and joust searching for the most apt metaphor to capture her mysterious beauty. Nefertiti and I watch as her limbs, which could have been lifted from the canvases of Botachelli rise and fall with her adoring sister's tender strokes.]

Nekeet: I am imagining I have run away from the palace to become a baker, your beauty is my precious, delicate pastry. I will knead you into our sweet bread of luck. With you, dear Sheeh, Egypt rises. {She laughs.}

Mye: Nekeet, shame on you. Have you been sleeping through your language lessons. You must find loftier metaphors to engage an elevated mind. Listen, 'As I touch you Sheeh, I am bathed in transcendence. Your balm cleanses me of all clandestine motives.'

Nekeet: {continuing to massage Sheeh} Your words float too high, Sheeh will have to scrape their meanings off papa's ceilings. 'Sheeh, touching you, soaks me in sweet mother's milk calming my chattering girl's tongue. Oiling your creamy loins turns my beaded sweat into rose perfume. Oh where will giving to you end?

Mye: Teach us fountain, from what source does such richness spring? How have you turned yourself into this flavor rack of pure spice? Is it for the love of Tatut that your love overflows?

Nekeet: Blasphemer! Sheeh has been trained in the Pharaoh's mysteries. The Aten's grace can be the only source of her other worldly light.

Mye: But, you've always been different Sheeh. Not aloof exactly but definitely apart and galaxies advanced. We are all masters, but you carry a separate light. You must teach us of your woman's mysteries. {She giggles} My voice sounds like papa's when he holds court.

Nekeet: I don't care where it comes from, I just want to be near you. Rubbing you, my hands turn into cocoa butter oars sailing me down a river of stars. You have an obligation to teach us, we are your blood sisters.

Mye: Yes, it's not fair, if it is not the Aten that fires your crystal eyes surely it is the love of a man.

Sheeh: As I give myself in deep surrender life's fire burns. It is her compassion's glow that lingers on my skin.

Mye: You do not say it is because of the Aten. Does this mean you would go against our father? He has done much good for Egypt. If its origin is not from union with him, tell us what supercedes his wisdom?

[Akenhaten enters suddenly, held up by two servants. He is dressed in a sheer gown. Sheeh rises from the table covering herself with her back turned as he watches, and then he beckons and she is lead into his new hall.]

Sheeh: Father, you watch me dress? Are yours the eyes I have sensed always upon me? Could it have been you all along? Don't you believe I will reflect in solitude what you have taught me? Have I not gladly lived out my youth in devotion, the recluse of your court? You violate me with your surveillance.

Akenhaten: I have waited patiently for your mind to mature under the guardianship of the Aten's light. You have been taken where no woman is permitted, into the initiate's sequestered chambers. You know more of enlightenment than a hundred queens. You alone have witnessed the ascension of my priests. It is my duty to monitor your coming of age. You are the female chosen by God's hierophant to lead the way for women. You are now ready to come onto the ship.

Sheeh: Is it you who has set your invisible prison around me, watching me all my life? Why do your eyes never give me rest?

I have loved you father, through long nights in meditation held together only by my belief in your 'ardent passion for truth.' I gave my youth to you gladly believing your teaching could comfort an ailing world. Tears fill her magnificent eyes. I remember when you proclaimed that 'beauty melded to purity' could one day grow into a brilliance equal to your own. I have worked to become that incarnation of faith through two decades of aloneness. My sisters do not know me. I have lost them to become your star, and now you do not protest when I accuse you of being my watcher?

Akenhaten: If you have been watched it is only by a father's protective eye. You are the female who God has chosen. You must not rob him of what I have toiled to fashion in his image. Would you deny me child?

Sheeh: Of course not father. But, tell me, what it is that I have not already given?

Akenhaten: Do not play coy with a king. Surely you have spoken with your sisters. Today I shall make you one with all that is. Today you shall receive all that you have been prepared to attain.

Sheeh: I am ready father, but how?

Akenhaten: Must I tell you what you already know?

I know your intelligence. I am certain your sisters have shared their joy.

Sheeh: My sisters have told me nothing.

Akenhaten: God directs me to be the vessel for his will. This you understand. You have seen his rebirth of Egypt before your eyes. Now it is your turn precious Sheeh. I have constructed this hall to his glory. Here I am directed to ordain you. On this obsidian bed you are destined to receive his blessings, like your sisters before you.

Sheeh: This is your "ardent passion for truth" father? This assault on women? To incest your own daughters? Who is this stranger before me once an inspired Pharaoh and devoted father? This cannot be he, lusting like a dog, stalking his own blood's virginity. Father listen to love's plea for your soul. Do not let life's sanctity drain from you and with it her blessings.

Akenhaten: Life, has taken herself from me long before I lay with my daughter's in bed. The soul she bleeds of vitality recharges itself upon God's alter.

Sheeh: Father, if you persist, it is here our futures part.

Akenhaten: Our future sings with the birds of dawn. We are their song to wake the sun. It is not possible for our futures to separate company.

Sheeh: You are mad father, and deeply deceived. I have been your loyalist student all these years. By you I have been taught that all else fades but the eternal heart. Purity and passion are the beams of your school I have taken within. I cannot topple. You see father, I did not understand her when the goddess warned me, in a premonition. It has taken years to pass, but when Tatut found me I was at once filled with your ardent passion. I did as I have always been instructed. I surrendered to it entirely. I let truth have me Father, the truth of my own love, of my own body's wisdom. You cannot take me, priest of the mighty Aten, for I, Sheeh, precious inheritor of your legacy have already been taken. It is your teaching that has saved me from you.

[Akenhaten flies into a rage, tearing down the drapes, kicking over the lanterns and artwork then falls, breaking her dressing table.]

Akenhaten: You cannot rob the prince of heaven. Virgin or not, it will never end here, daughter. Here it begins! It is not my eye that is your spy, but his all-seeing presence. A love this great can know nothing short of satisfaction.

Sheeh: Have you educated me to be no more than ripened goddess fruit readied to be plucked by rage? The beauty you desire to possess is of the inner self, a crystal polished by daily acts of love and care. Life evolves only through those that can be trusted not to violate her integrity, Father.

Akenhaten: Her integrity? What integrity is this, random chaos polluted and peppered with agony? Come out with me child. I have found a way. Why am I, Pharaoh, bringing the new word from heaven if life does not require my God for her transformation?

Sheeh: You are tolerated as her transitional guardian only because no one will listen to women any longer. You have made us unbelievable, casting our sacredness out of your temples. I had hoped to temper your will, but I see now you are no more than a liar, surrounding yourself with mother and my sisters. You pretend equality in public, but we are no more than blurred symbols by your side. I cannot be loyal to an incestor.

Akenhaten: Mankind cannot progress from a wisdom spoken out of the moody mouths of woman. You were my model for her reformation. Now there will be none.

Sheeh: Incest would make me ready for service? To what father? My woman's mind is ruled by heart as complex as the cycles of renewing life, as intricate as the natural world's interdependencies. What you have done to my sisters turns you into a dead man. You are destroying those who could return you to the sensations of the living. You have left me no other choice than to grow separate from you, to heal the error of this atrocious crime. Father you will be left feeling nothing and those who stand by you will become impotent, evaporating like dew with the noon sun. No trace of your rich maleness will remain, save the wounds that you leave behind for us to heal.

Akenhaten: I want nothing of the diabolical sensations of crippled flesh. Existence is the hell careless mothers caste me into. Do not go against me, Sheeh. You give me no choice but to punish you as God would for your disloyalty. I will cut you from your love Tatut. I will hunt you and separate you from his ecstasy until you respect the will of your father. You will be lost from your soul's mate. I will not allow you to reunite. I have the power to do this at my command. Lifetimes of aloneness and pain await you if you oppose me. You will be a debtor until you settle your account. Is it worth all this not to come unto my house? And, make no mistake daughter, if you awaken women to your cause I will bring you down with more oppression than the poorest peasant girl has ever dreamed. You will be denied resources to accomplish your mutinous goals. I am the law behind all religions that spring from the father. As war rages between men, through their cries for death you shall hear me call your name. Hear me, for the hound I now let loose will track your scent for eternity. If ever there comes a time when the world considers your woman's awakening, I will be the muzzle to keep that bitch in heat, constrained in duality. She will not find the voice of truth with her tongue sewn with your mutiny. As she presumes power, she will draw up the energy of my rage. If she sets out to be priestess, again, she will only incense a humanity I claim for the father, with her yapping pups. I have been sent to retrieve immortality. Men and their women will quake with suspicion if you return, seeking to reform the world I have made with your emotional mind. When they feel what has become of you they will beg for rebirth in the logic of the one father god. We span millennium.

Nefertiti: He could not seduce her with his perversion and it drove him wild. Look at him, flailing like a downed quail, pissing on himself as he dies before her in his coward's act of suicide.

Akenhaten: I will never let you go Sheeh, I cannot. This does not end here, here it begins!

BLACKOUT

Chapter

17

I awoke with Act II intact, racing through my throbbing head. By my bloodied toes, a note saying goodnight and thanking me for <u>Shemura and her Men</u> had been pushed under the door. Relieved, Charlotte and Janis had left without incident, I rose slowly from the golden veined bathroom floor. Dodging the broken glass, I tore open the cupboards searching for my first aid kit and something to sweep up the chards. As I brushed them into the dustpan they scattered like shreds of a treasure map, never meant to be pieced back together. I hobbled past my digital travel clock, wondering how long I'd been out. Its jumbled numbers displayed only unintelligible symbols caught in the unmarked zones of timelessness. It was fried. I searched for my pen then, as I sat at my desk eager to transcribe scene II, my ballpoint flew from my grasp hitting the patio window and shattering the sliding glass door. Glass was again everywhere. The night air swept into my room and with it the chilling certainty that these two love goddesses, Sheeh and Shemura were one and the same. Struggling to catch my breath, I felt I had brought Akenhaten's rage back with me. It thundered, electrically opposing my awakening understanding.

As my breath calmed, I closed my eyes, praying for truth, strength and clear vision. I remembered my last visit with Shemura, sitting in her country home, surrounded by beds of flowers waiting for a free moment to be planted, along with mounds of paperwork. Piled on her desk were proposals to launch her dream, a revolutionary community of women committed to seeding programs to help birth a new humanity, rich with new vision, feminine intelligence and creative passion. She was creating a think tank for women's future, summoning the world's most dedicated females to co-author a compassionate restructuring of society. Our research at Kingsgate was meant to be the start up capital to fund her network of remarkable women, all expert "paradigm busters" ready to restore balance to a world still marred with far too much oppression and abuse.

Was now the time Akenhaten warned Sheeh of? If so, it was not he but I who was endangering her mission. I was the one threatening to ruin Shemura's reputation. It was my mishandling of our patient at Kingsgate Psychiatric Hospital that froze her funding. It was I who allowed Riley to become the tragic pawn in Akenhaten's game. If the Pharaoh's desire to possess Sheeh was his bow was I not his arrow, poised to hit Shemura with his mark? How could this be? How could a woman do this to the cause of all women?

I rummaged through my tiny fridge, finding some walnuts, apples, Brie, and a few crackers. Then I moved outside to ask my questions through the eternity reflected within the stillness of the desert night.

"Was it true? Could my life be motivated by the madness of an Egyptian Pharaoh dead four thousand years? If I was Akenhaten's tool to destroy Shemura and her mission then how did his predatory urge live inside of me? Nefertiti had made it clear we were one and the same. How does a man's destructive energy live inside his woman? What has pulled me into their stream of abuse?" No answers came, only a gentle breeze and with it the feeling my questions where enough for now.

When I returned the inside of the room was still moist and hot with Akenhaten's rage. It was as though he were tracking me, ready to battle me if I went against him. I hurriedly dressed, hoping to get out from under his fury and the feeling he would stop at nothing to possess Shemura and stop her mission.

At the main desk I reported the broken glass then decided to sit for a spell in the bar by the pool. Ordering a Brandy Alexander I sipped deeply, my goblet catching the shimmers off the tangerine pool lights. Their rays skittered through my shaking hands to dance on the water. Drinking in their light I felt relieved. My mouth filled with the taste of the pomegranates she had been served as his queen. I felt the silk Akenhaten must have ordered for her from far away China, to drape her illustrious torso. I inhaled the frankincense and musk she burned in his temples and as I leaned back in my chair the crown that mankind placed upon her head as a symbol of their trust pressed into my temples. I was inseparably one with Nefertiti, bound within the lineage of her emotional history. Humanities bounty hunter had found me at last. I was to live with the energetic experience of the evil she had succumbed to until it was no more. This is what was being asked of me. This was the reason I had come to Shambhala.

As the stars broke through the cloud covered azure sky my childhood's fire dragon filled my body. I suddenly felt my Uncle's incest had been compensation for lifetimes of heartlessness and, a tool to deliver me back under Akenhaten's will. I felt a familiar stubbornness to have my way, I had re-enacted lifetime after lifetime. I experienced myself many, many times taking what I wanted at the expense of others. This pattern of selfishness must have drawn his intent to me again and again. I had served him before. I closed my eyes and asked when it began. I felt myself as a dynamic high priestess sitting high in an ancient temple. Hordes of horses and soldiers with swords and torches were destroying my land and burning our temples. My sister healers were raped, sodomized and tortured. I escaped their fate by going with these men and doing what they asked of me. I gave them what they wanted, my psychic talents helped them plot the best occasions to attack the unsuspecting. I held still bringing myself deeper into the past. He was there. His vendetta against women joined these invaders and rode inside their inflamed psyche to bring down the worship of the feminine as divine in many parts of the world. He came for me through the wave of their mass assault and I went with him to protect myself, To save myself I united with their campaign. It drove me into something deeper that I still could not grasp wielded from the world of magic and energetic psychic control. Because of the strength I possessed he sought me out. Nefertiti needed me now to break what she was calling his curse. But what is a curse but an energetic hold that one cannot break free of?

I opened my tear filled eyes to see the pool's waterfall streaming with visions of fallen flowers tumbling down its wall of rocks. Each had the face of one of Nefertiti's darling girls. Mora, appeared melancholy and mysterious, encouraging me to accept the truth of these lifetimes that somersaulted before me, to bring justice to her and her sisters so that their inestimable contribution would not remain kidnapped forever.

As Mora's image began to fade I heard her say "Mama, the library. We were erased. Find us." Then she was gone. I did not know Shambhala had a huge metaphysical library. Mora's spirit had come to help me take my next step. I spent the early morning ensconced in its suede rocking chair, reading everything I could about their dynasty. Inside the huge Mahogany hall lit in full spectrum light, I learned Queen Nefertiti was considered Akenhaten's co-regent. And, he was remembered as a supporter of women! History shrouded his sexual appetites, painting him as a misunderstood superhero. I could find no account, whatsoever, of his hatred of women. He left his mark as a man that upheld his wife and family. Although it was known he had more than one wife, Queen Nefertiti was portrayed as his equal. She had disappeared mysteriously, as had he. Archeologists at this very moment were on a quest to unearth their mummies. Nefertiti's bust has endured as a symbol of woman's spiritual authority and beauty. The details of her reign are one of the world's great mysteries.

I laughed out loud, causing the other esoteric students to scowl from under their mystical texts.

Akenhaten's spiritual legacy was pristine. He was credited with being the priest who brought the world's religions out of a dark age. Right now authorities on Egypt and mysticism, including a popular world wide ancient mystical order, stemming from his religion, espouse the royal duo were misunderstood, enlightened, world leaders. They are esteemed as pioneers who evolved the spiritual consciousness for all mankind. It was a huge cover up!

A wave of discouragement swept through me, if I tried to expose the nightmare of perverse energy and intent that poured through me linked to the royal pair I would never be believed. Energy does not lie, but in a world that, for the most part, still doesn't acknowledge such energies even exist who would believe me? Who would accept Akenhaten was right now seeking to control the future through women like myself? What was I to do with such knowledge? I was battling more than a perversion that hide behind mankind's yearning for a papa protector God, I was fighting those that wanted to keep the myth of his priestly purity alive.

"Are you all alone?" a voice inquired, just as I was about to get up to leave.

"Yes, I am." I responded to the woman who then asked if I wanted company. She was wearing a colorful turban and bright-layered clothes with a long swaying skirt and armfuls of vibrant bracelets. Her dark skin highlighted the brightness of the whites of her eyes. I was afraid she was another of Yogicar's women

137

but she assured me she was on her own, and that tonight was a very special night.

"Cum out to da patio and have a drink." She said. Exhausted and bleak, I followed her to the poolside bar where I was startled to find it was once again night.

"She be gatherin, gatherin, gatherin. Billions of years jus fur right now! Isn't dat spectacoolar? We blessed to be alive!" She spoke in a thick accent I thought at first to be Jamaican.

"Excuse me, my name is Natalie Stearn and you are...?" I asked, my suspicion overriding her enthusiasm.

"Ruby, I talk to dead peple? Dat scare you?" she smiled.

"Yes" I replied.

"Yu too no?" she said laughing.

"No I just hangout with them. I'm sorry, I'm very upset tonight. You're welcome to stay, but I'm not likely to be much fun."

"You wan a readin? For you I do for free, because of da night." She smiled so broadly I couldn't resist.

"What night?" I asked as she unwrapped an emerald green velvet satchel and laid out her deck. It was written in an antiquated French calligraphy. Sighing and talking to herself she took my hand and shook her head.

"You are a dark sista, but evul can turn good. Yu just gatherin the strength then boom you gonna drop da bomb. You got a frend dun most da work already. She taught you everything, now the eart appear in person maybe you listen now? Da Eart set to free a lot a women. You owe it to em. Betta get finished wit dat buk. Why yu so miserable? Don't you know you are dis cloz to fweedom?"

"I may have gone along with something for too long that is impossible for me to reverse." I said with desperation in my voice.

"Yu got no faith. Ain't seein true. Eart ain't takin dis no more. Look here big powful man," she said throwing the hierophant card onto the table.

"Yu shakin! Why you believe in him when da eart bout to push his stuff right out a here? She changin herself intu a great star. No more men lik dat telling her children how high to jump. Love coming from out dar," she pointed to the stars and laughed as a feeling of happiness seemed to shine down clearing my somber mood with a mist from the spiraling nebula above us. Love pourin in, into da mama's belly. She goin too high to let dem get her dat low ever gain. It all be changing, an fast. Yu got to read in-between da lines at all dat bad news. Da great mama spirit dat make everythin is lightin up da earth wit love. We right here wit her, feelin her. She stronger den any a us. She got da force to blast it all out a us, but we got to choose it. We got to bring it out den she want to clear it up." As she spoke she directed me to look up again. I had never seen more stars clearly etched in the heavens.

"Oh you sooo fraid at dat old boy. Yu pull it outta da women and children you pull it outta da future.

I asked her if she would like a drink and when she pointed to mine I ordered her one.

"Stop feelin soo sorry for yurself. You went long with it long time! Lot a hard work comin, but alot of dancin and playin too. Can't you feel da energy?"

"This energy is not at all playful." I retorted.

"Oh she know all bout dat, we all been dare." Her forehead narrowed as she threw the empress card out.

Don't da Eart talk to you? Don't she try to lift you up, to clear dis out of you, so you can help da others get over it too? You got a frend teach you this, and you write about it, but you don't get it. Yu don't see why yu got to write yur book, tellin such a bad story ta people dats already mizrable. You fraid da ain't gonna want to go down into da dark, but you don't see da healin in dat."

"I'm not writing a book. I'm only transcribing a play that's coming to me at different times."

"You will, you will."

"Who would want to go where this journey is taking me? People want to be lifted up."

"Ya right. People is wantin to feel good, but how they gonna do dat witout pulling dis crap out a dem? Ya don't understand da memory. It's da time clock tickin inside da tissue of man. Its da story dat keeps repeatin. How long ya story been playin on doz lousy moovy theaters insid people's blood? Yu ain't da only one suffrin wit da same misrable story playin over 'n over gain. You show it to da peple and da eart help dem get over it. Yu writin pull it up, but its da eart wit da womun un childrun gunna bring in da new energy." She lifted her hands skyward with a peaceful grin. "You come tonight to da canyon and see."

Ruby took my hand and led me to her jeep in the parking lot out front. I did nothing to stop her.

"Yu cum now. Dis is da nit grat love comin down. Da sisters danz it down into da eart by mornin eart clean da blood, da cells, da memory, yu see."

"Shemura is the only healer I trust to help, but I can't get near her with this, it's directed at her."

"Da mama, she fur everyone."

Do you mean no matter how dark I have become it can be cleared from the cellular memory with the earth's help?"

"Yes dats it. Now you got it. Nothin too dark for da mama. She like da dark sistas when they come right cause they pack a punch. Don't be runnin. Truth chase you like a wildcat at matin seasun. Tear you apart before you know she on you." She shuddered seeing something she refused to voice.

" Dats why womun needs to write hur books. Books frum da knawed heart, da crushed bone marrow, da strangled throat, crazy books dat no one wan beleevs but da got to."

"Why do they have to?" I asked perplexed.

"Cause somethin ring too true in da body where da mama talk to 'em. Day got too much for da heads already firin up the brain. Too much a dat make da kids take up da guns."

By the time we arrived at the clearing covered in sand paintings we were painted with desert sand ourselves.

"Dis is da place to let all da poison out. Don't matter how old, the time come to play. Mama loves da play."

Just as Ruby had told me, back at Shambhala, elders and children were playing together in a way I had never seen, painting while others played games, cooked and built a open fire-pit. I could feel how important the very young and elderly had become to one another out here.

"I don't remember ever seeing young people wanting to spend much time with old folks. What's going on here?" I asked.

" You see when yu old you be just like childrun gain."

After a few relaxed hours passed everyone joined hands, singing and dancing dressed in costumes that made music with layers of hanging shells.

"Now daa took good care a each udder daa ready to let in what da earth give em. Ruby lead us to sit at their open fire. The heat of their hearth drew up waves of fever and chills as the orange moon rose like a fireball over the steep canyon's ridge. The comfort of sustained tones held us steadfast as a flute echoed against the canyon walls, to the slow beat of the dancer's deer skin drums. The heaviness of the past weeks lifted from some central channel of being that exploded out of the top of my head and then I was on fire with a whiteness that burned me like hot coals. Inside their circle the women and children tugged at a rope held by a man in a fur robe covered with tin cans.

"Who is that?" I asked, scarcely able to speak.

"He da same dum guy been controlin and destroyin things too long an da women an elders and children be tied up wit em too long."

The robed figure dragged them across the field. They wailed and moaned, trying to steady each other. Their cries brought goosebumps to my icy flesh. I was reminded of all the innocent victims of power. Then a figure surrounded him coming from all four directions. Women dressed in handmade capes encircled him and began to chant.

Ruby explained that each woman spirit restores a different aspect of the force of creation he brought into the darkness. She said we learned to hold onto him for safety and comfort because he controlled most of the world's money and resources, but it was time to let go of the men of power.

"Women scared for da children stay wit da man. Time to leav da man, yu know when time is to let go. Yu got to do it."

The children and women scurried under the capes of the wise old sisters, leaving him alone. I watched as the earth began to drain the poison from me. He sat like a fallen humpty dumpty, all by himself. They did not hurt or punish him, they just let go of his rope and joined another fire where they all danced and laughed and held each other close. All night they exuded the intoxication of play. Ruby joined them, encouraging me to follow her, but I did not feel well enough nor did I feel that I belonged yet in their circle. I watched feeling within myself that my contracts with power separated me from them as they drew light up from the earth's luminous womb, celebrating her stardom with their stomping bare feet. Their bodies did things I had never seen bodies do before. They arched so far to the ground I thought their spines would crack in half but they had no rigidity. Every piece of them smiled as they swayed with surrender, sharing their pleasure as streams of light rose from the earth, visible even to my naked eye.

"How can this be; I am so ill and they are so... ?" I struggled to find the words for what I saw.

"Tonit a new energy com. Dis com to help da future. Dis sta now and get stronger every day. See all da help? See all da energy? Sum peoples belev in the earth energy. Yu open up da wound and da mama clean da energy. Dunt be fraid to go deep inta da dark, yu clean up da wound she heal up da energy. Tu simple for da complex brain a man but da women and da children and da elders day feel it."

These unlikely partners of very young and old danced until their sweat dissolved the sand painted images beneath their feet while Ruby and the others sang:

Dat be da prayer to da mama.
Da mama a all life protect da man
but if he go against her tu many times she take em out.
She brought em in
An she take him out.
She brings him in
An she can take him out.

I rubbed my eyes in disbelief as images of violence, aggression and pain like spirits rose from the dancers and were burned by the light. They fell like stardust into the sand, beaten gently back into the earth. The dancers grew more and more luminescent until I could not see their physicality at all. They were luminous light beings.

"Da mama of all life brought him in an she will take him out."

She looked deep and shook her head. "You still got a lot a crap in dar. All da energy from all da power since dat queen let dat Pharaoh steal da moon, gonna take some time to clean all dat crap out, but you get there. And dat guy of hers, he gonna fight ya to da end. But dats now. You can't stay for da rest a it, yu got to clean dis up first den we see yu gain."

She drove me back to Shambhala, singing all the way, while I shook wetting her seat covers with my sweat.

When she dropped me off she hugged me and said, "We all got to find da way alon. Thousands a seekers don't get to see what you seen tonit." I asked her if there was a way I could contact her and she agreed. I went inside to get a pen but when I returned she was gone. When I asked the concierge which direction she had headed he insisted I had arrived alone, that he had seen no one with me. Inside I queried the bar maid if she remembered the woman who sat with me the night before. She said I had passed the night alone and insisted my bar tab had only one Brandy Alexander on its stub. Walking back to my room I realized I did not know where we had driven. I had not even asked what Indian tribe performed this Earth ritual. The information center had no record of any local tribes scheduling such a gathering anywhere near Las Madrinas. They assured me that they kept a close eye on such happenings. I was baffled but in no way could discount what I had been given that night.

"Da energy, it real." I heard Ruby say. "Da energy, it real."

I wrapped myself in an Indian blanket I had found in my closet. Sitting in meditation all morning I felt my body pulse with the joy I had been privileged to experience.

Too weak to move off my sofa I decided to switch on the television for the first time since I had arrived. A blank faced twenty year old was smothering herself in lotion promising that if I did the same I would defy the deterioration of my collagen. All day I drifted in and out of consciousness burning then freezing, waking briefly to women giving testimony to the miracles of a vaginal crème that drove the odor of their sex underground. With mean spirited pouting expressions on their faces, they forced their breasts into bras that pushed their nurturing domes up into the faces of energy-starved men.

By midnight I ripped the television from the wall. Still swaying with Ruby, dancing in the open field, strong with life's grace, I hungered to find any tiny spark that could match their light. But, I would need help. Someone that could understand the struggle I was engaged in and the forces that opposed it. The only person who fit that description was Gary. I had to go back to him.

Chapter

18

The bus ride out to Gary's casita was long and hot. Dust clung to the late spring cactus flowers paling their celebration. My pleated Indian dress clung to me as I nervously searched the painted desert for the first signs of the pyramids. I was concerned that I might not be welcomed back at Gary's. After all the care he gave me, I had been rude, leaving so abruptly.

"Don't expect me to hike back to them pyramids look'in for you this time. First off I don't buy into none a that, second, I got a bad knee." Miraim chided. "I called out three times that night for you Dr. Stearn. How was I supposed to know that a snake bit you? You coulda got me fired, staying so long, sick an all. You could a sent that loony toons out to the road to tell me what was goin on. You sure you want to go out there again? There's a rattler under every rock in the heat a the day. Don't say I didn't warn ya."

"Thank you. I'm sure I'll be fine. I don't intend for another snake to bit me."

"You sure you're a psychologist? You think anyone intends to be bit by a rattler? Excuse me for going off, but I get fed up with all this mumbo jumbo. Now here comes another lot. How did a whole generation of young people get so screwed up? That's what I wanna know. Skip-id-y-du-da here we go again. Young things decked out in flimsy togas leaving their tear-soaked wads-a-Kleenex all over my bus. Can't hardly bend down to pick 'em up. See that bundle over there?" She said shaking her head and pointing under the cowhide seats.

"How'm I supposed to dig all that out? Every trip a new bunch of them is leaving then coming back, then leaving again. What's Shambhala turned into a home for runaway loonies? That's what I wanna know. I'm too old to play truant officer to a bunch a spaced out grandchildren, I got enough of my own."

Sitting next to her I wished she was not so testy and I could tell her why I was making my pilgrimage, like one of Yogicar's exiles.

I said my good-byes, reassuring her I would be more cautious this trip. Then I snuck past her, out the folding bus doors as the afternoon clouds mounted the sun, like a gang of reckless cowboys. She called to me as I waved farewell running down the path to Gary's.

"Don't forget now, I ain't gonna look for ya this time, so you best take care of your own sweet self, ya hear me?"

As I approached Gary's casita I wondered why a sophisticated center like Shambhala kept Miriam on.

"Does the smell of grease still make you nauseous?" Gary asked, standing in the doorway, barefoot in his jean over-alls and chef's apron.

"No, well not unless your serving eggs serpentine." We both doubled over with laughter, like two estranged childhood friends, reunited.

"I hope you're in the mood for some radiant sensuality, Italian style. You're just in time for my specialty, Eggplant Parmesan." Gary said cheerfully. His casita smelled like little Italy at Christmastime. Garlic and tomato sauce, onions and oregano, cilantro and olive oil crackled on his stove, braided with the aroma of toasted almond and vanilla biscotti's. I was sure he would be angry with me or worse. He seemed just fine all by himself, cooking up his fresh garden vegetables and old world pastry. Pulling out a wicker chair he gestured like a maitre- de for me to sit down. Then he eased the cork off a chilled bottle of Chianti. He lit the room with scented clove and cinnamon candles then came closer, draping his spindle table with a red and white-checkered cloth. When he sat by my side we ate with a silent intensity.

His casserole melted on my palate, sending an armistice into the war zone of my flesh.

"The Raven is your totem you know, not the snake." He pronounced. "Look up there."

Through his window a solitary raven squawked. The sound came from a tree that cast shadows on us, like spider legs. It was only when he turned down the flame warming the remaining eggplant and pulled his stool to my other side, that I saw the lacerations on his eyes and wrists.

"What happened to you? Has someone broken in again?" I asked.

"No. Don't worry Natalie. Periodically I do this to myself. It's happened all my life. That's why I live alone, so no one else is made responsible."

"You did this to yourself?"

"I've been hospitalized a bunch of times. I just don't want to take their medication. I can't write my songs on that stuff. It's better out here, in the country. The spirits keep me sane, most of the time. I've never actually lit myself on fire but I think about it a lot, you know what dying that way would be like, the hot flames lapping up my flesh, churning the air into ash. I just don't like the part about knowing I could leave here completely incomprehensible. Don't worry. Now that the moons full it'll pass. I need her to break through. The moons far more reliable than the Sun. She responds.

147

You can count on her for that. Will you stay and take a Jacuzzi with me? Did you see my new hot tub out back?"

"What hot tub?"

"The one I built this week in case you returned. Actually, I was sure you would. He told me so." He said pointing to the raven that was staring straight at us through the curtained window.

"He likes it when we're together. He gets to be right. He told me we were a match. Do you have a taste for bathing in wild lavender under the moonlight?"

If I were another sort of person, I would have made any excuse not to stay until I knew I was not dangerous to others. Instead, I settled into the warmth I craved from the man who was waiting to take care of me.

The hot tub was in a cluster of ancient Pines. Las Madrinas' wonderland of high desert forest formed a ring of deep green embracing arms around us. Gary wrapped me in his towel, then as the moon rose like a giant ball of lemon crème, we floated, relaxing in the amber light. His mood suddenly sobered as he spoke of the struggle of his adolescence, seduced down New York's back streets with addicts who introduced him to their brand of alley sex.

"There," he said pointing to the side of one of the pyramids where the temple stairs seemed to end. "Those monks are no different. They're far from holy. They play on my frustration. I know its my own weakness that let's them in. I've spent too many nights letting strangers reach into my pants. What made me keep going back for more? I don't get it, there was no love in it. What happened, Natalie? Why did you run off?"

Touched by the raw intimacy of his confession, I reached for my backpack and pulled out my transcript. He laid back and read the scene between Akenhaten and Sheeh. Then whispered, "Bastard, what a sick bastard. Sheeh, she's got to be your friend. Natalie, she's Shemura. I can feel it."

"How do you know that?" I questioned as his whole body began to tremble.

"This is real. It all really happened. Didn't it?" He said with an uncanny certainty. "This must be why they're so angry. Those hooded monks are going nuts. They never thought you'd get as far as you have."

"Why do you say that?"

"I just know it. They don't want this to be revealed. They come here every night. Their chanting is planting holograms into the vortex. They know this place will send their nasty control all over the place. And then there's you coming back. That's got to be something they knew would happen. These Egyptian power brokers play outside of time."

"Why are you so certain they have anything to do with me or Akenhaten?" I asked, not convinced that Gary's visions and my life were running that parallel. "Lots of religions have monks and most of them wear hoods."

"You don't think they're the same ones who have been with you since you were a kid?" He asked, his face flushed with the desire to be believed.

"You know I could have just imagined them, to keep things interesting with Horowitz. His form of psychoanalysis was pretty boring stuff for a young woman to live through. I'm a dramatist. I always have been. I exaggerate and embellish everything."

"But you were able to return to Egypt without the venom or the antidote? Bravo! Don't you see how incredible this valley is? It's a true portal. I knew you could do it! Your time here, with me, has opened you hasn't it?"

"I don't know, maybe. It was a freak accident really, I got knocked out. Just as I was losing consciousness she came for me. When I sat down to write it all down my pen flew out of my hand and broke the sliding glass door. It felt as though Akenhaten's rage came back with me."

"Go back into the temple with me Natalie. We can find out why they arrived the same time you did. We can get them to stop what there doing. It's not good for this place or anyone." He took hold of my hand then his eyes softened "I'm sorry, I'm sure that's the very last thing you want. That last trek up the pyramid nearly killed you." He took my hands and held them tightly to his chest. "Our connection isn't about all the details, it's just here, like the craters of the moon. It may sound crazy, but my life is useless until I am discovered, until I am called to love, to love a woman."

As he kissed me we shook with unspoken recognition. Then his body rose, shimmering with beads of water turned golden in the moonlight.

"They're not helping love. It's only getting worse. They chant all night. The whole valley gets so polluted when there's no wind I have to sleep in the hot tub. It's the only place I feel protected. I wish I was stronger."

"Oh Gary," I broke in hoping to shift his mood. "I wish you could have been there the other night." I met a woman, Ruby, she read my cards and brought me out somewhere to a tribe of wonderful people. My visions and voices, she said it was the Divine Mother, the Earth speaking directly to me. The strange thing is, after I returned inside Shambhala to look for a pen, to get her phone number she was gone. Then everyone insisted I had never been with her, but I know she was there."

"Oh Ruby, yes, superlative apparition. The Rainbow Tribe is real enough. They jump dimensions. Ruby appears with messages. Congratulations! It's a fantastic affirmation of what you're trying to accomplish. The Earth is a being, Natalie, count on it. Conscious, just like you or me. Of course no one really believes that here except the Indians and crazy people like us.

"The Rainbow Tribe's been here a couple a times. I'm sure they're the only reason this valley clears out fast enough for me to survive, sometimes. They embody the future, one heart, uniting every race on earth, a true coming together of every nationality and religion. They are working directly with the earth for the transformation.

I don't know, I just feel it's her, it's all her, the Earth, however we let her in. She loves us so much. She comes in on any ray of sincerity we give her. You know, that lost place, that link to all that is sacred, that no one sees but it's the only connection that keeps you alive? For me, it's like if someone doesn't get that's all that really matters to me soon, I'm going to just crack. Then there she is, sliding right in, like a Boeing 747, emergency landing on my soul's black ice runway. 'Here it is kid, hang on. You've had a rough ride but help is on the way.' Why else would Ruby have just shown up in your life, when you were afraid you couldn't take another breath? And afterwards, when I'm fine again, poof she just disappears." He was smiling, soothed in the radiance of the Earth's love.

It was then that I prayed for him. When I opened my eyes I saw the trees' branches reaching like the great mother's arms to rekindle the balance in this sensitive, immediate man. I felt her gently guiding us together. Our separate journeys had prepared us. We were molten wax poured from her lava caldron, changing into two sand candles. It is as if we were meant to light each other's way out from where we had lost ourselves to a perverse sexuality.

"Let's not talk about this anymore," he said kissing my neck and shoulders, applying lavender oil to my muscles, coiled with fear.

The canyon echoed our sighs, in a choir of celebration, as he offered himself to me. He engaged his passion nobly, but it was a battle. It seemed as though, with each touch someone were trying to seduce him away.

He harnessed the whole of his concentration just to remain present. He gave with a colossal sensuality, a heroic sexuality that refused to rest until he consummated my pleasure. The sincerity of his desire drove us deep into a shared mythology. His brown eyes dilated into two huge saucers, as did mine. I let go into his arms and we slid out of this world. He transformed the water into holy robes enfolding me. I was Jerusalem's harlot, as he dragged me to safety, away from a jeering mob. He kissed the blood from my neck, drawn by jealous stones that pelted my whore's body. His lips sutured my wounds with light. We shuddered, crying out like exorcists casting out evil spirits.

"Every Easter Sunday I meditate and kind of re-live the life of Jesus." He said. "I go through all the stations of the cross. It just happens. I don't want it to. It's so painful, but I can't stop it. It's like Jesus lives through me as the real man He was. Like I'm supposed to get it and let the world know he wasn't what they have made Him out to be. It sounds crazy but He wants to come back, even through guys like me, to help people heal from something that's been done to them. He was meant to redefine male spirituality by being a sacred lover."

Under the pyramids' dark shadow my supple lover offered me his version of Holy Communion. No sexless martyr, he pronounced with each wild, deep, playful stroke "I am the love of woman." I waited for his next touch like the exhale waits for breath. If I had let him, his love could have erased every memory I had to remain bitter. He was my redeemer and I his Mary Magdalene. He did not care that I lay in his pool, sweating, with no make-up, and no decency. He did not chastise me for where my sex had been, nor that I had abandoned my female spirit, to wander the world, an empty predator.

His love shook it loose. Darkness rose to pull us back to misery. But this night it's vile, intimidation did not stop love. He looked straight into it and did not shrink away. It was disarmed and recoiled, letting up the seeds of the gentle woman I longed to become. Gary opened the portal to my nurturing goodness. With each thrust our love making affirmed the virility of his tenderness. The openness of his tender, patient fire was restoring me to life.

He said, "You are so beautiful, I want to be with you." I could not believe anyone would ever say such words to me. But it was true. I was beautiful, like every woman who allows love to over-ride her destructivity. By daybreak his passion had created an astounding rescue. His love had washed us clean. We rested on the desert shore of love's pure intent.

Plain sand, no cabanas by the pool, the ground zero of love, the sprout bursting from the dung heap of love's betrayals, the fibroblast, criss-crossing the open wounds of loss, the freedom after terror.

"This is how worlds are formed' I cried out.

"And how living in them is meant to feel." he responded.

He fanned the glimmer of my compromised female spirit with soft kisses until the moon left us to sleep, our arms intertwined like rosary beads suspended in prayers of peace.

Chapter

19

"I'm going for a walk," I whispered, blowing kisses into Gary's dreams as he slept. Restless, unable to wait for him to awake, I reluctantly pulled myself from him.

"Don't leave," he sighed wiping his lips with my curls. "Don't forget the raven." Before I could ask him what I was to remember, his breath let go to the deep rhythms of slumber, releasing me to embrace the day alone.

I dressed slowly, savoring my memories of this minstrel's lovemaking, sending warm currents up my thighs. I danced over the night's bath towels, and then spun the Aztec warrior statue that Gary kept for protection by the front door, ballroom style, until my toes tingled.

Outside, the sun had not yet baked the dew off his raised garden of herbs that glowed with welcome. I licked the moisture from his mint and basil, letting my recollection of his sensuality wash me onto the shores of a fresh day. Breathing in the bouquet of lemon sage that burst open on the lazy morning rays of sunlight I heard these

words singing in my mind, "Give thanks upon the pyramid's peak."
The divine essence some called God which I knew now only as life,
was picking me up from where Gary had taken me, allowing me
safe return from my devouring past. I thought I heard Ruby's voice,
"Da earth she talkin to ya. It time yu lisun."

Gratefully I climbed the crumbling pyramid's steps. From the
top I could see a second then, a third smaller rock pyramid,
camouflaged by trees. The three created a triangle on the canyon
floor. This must be the apex point of the vortex, I marveled. As
I wondered who had built these shrines, a sound entered my
head. Was the vortex amassing her magnificent force now to
help me grow the seed woman of last night grounded in this new
day? I spread myself out on the altar top to savor the earth's
pulse along with my memories of re-birth. The tones grew more
intense, making me almost giddy with enthusiasm. My whole
body vibrated. Then, as though I had not been given sign or
miracle enough, I was lifted off the altar, like Nefertiti's daughters.
It was an indescribable thrill! My hands rose, ready to do the
bidding of this exuberant presence. I was being lifted to the azure
heavens!

Waves of bliss held me suspended in euphoria and then I
was advised, "Be grateful for what has come to you through this
young man. Take the message, not the messenger. Beware though
he has unlocked a great blessing he will just as quickly release a
great despair to threaten your emerging truth." Then it ceased,
and before I could respond I was once more swept away in what
seemed a choir of angels.

I floated for hours, loving my gravity-less box seat at this
unexpected cosmic symphony. I would have passed the whole
of the day levitating in the sun if the raven had not alerted me.
Squawking and circling it broke the magic's hold. Disoriented, I
looked to find a way down the western slope when the bird
landed on the other side, scolding me. I walked over to meet
him. But when I could almost touch his wing, he flew west
again where a dust storm, barely visible, was roughing up the tundra

below. He bolted from me flying and screeching down the shrine until he turned himself into a tiny speck of jet black, liting on Gary's chain fence, filling the valley with his screeches.

I felt drugged descending the sloping stone, only half cognizant of what I had heard. As I eyed the pyramid that only a few days before had sent me down its craggy slopes, I did not want to see I was walking down nothing more than a natural rock formation! It was not made by any man. Las Madrinas had carved what crumbled under my moccasins over billions of years. The structure was layered in clearly visible archeological stratums of stone. At the base there were no antechambers, no doors, no secret rooms, and no chanting monks. Gary was wrong. The warning was right and I was about to make another fatal error if I did not listen. I did not want to believe what I was being shown, that Gary was a strange muddle of strength and weakness too unpredictable, too unstable, and although for moments glorious, I could not believe him. My heart hurt with alarm, but what could I do?

When I returned to his casitia Gary rushed at me like a lost puppy, following me from room to room. I had to ask him to leave me alone just to use his bathroom. He was about to make a grocery run, but kissing my ankles, down on his knees, he changed his mind and begged me to make the trip for him.

"You have a vehicle? Where is it hidden…under the hen's house?" I joked, trying to conceal my grief.

"No, over there." He said pointing to the storage shed that was not a shed at all but his dented Ford pick-up covered in a torn and faded army surplus tarp.

"I don't drive it much. I have anxiety attacks just thinking of leaving here most of the time." He explained.

"Where's town?" I inquired.

"Not far," He said drawing me a map. " Do you mind? I am not ready for the zoo today."

"The zoo?" I retorted, hoping to get out before he caught me eyeing his inadequacies.

"Oh Las Madrinas is crawling with wanna be light seekers and

157

tourists snapping their pictures, I just can't take it. They always want me to sing them my stuff. I'm not up to it."

"But what about the dust storm?"

"Don't worry, as much as I have wanted to lose myself in one, they never amount to much. I haven't seen one materialize in years. If you remember, could you pick up some extra candles, just in case we are lucky enough to match our passion with a whopper storm tonight? You will stay another night won't you?" He asked pressing me to his chest. Then my dark Adonis bit my nipple through my muslin blouse, using his mouth like a bass player's fingers searching for the perfect note; the note that would evoke last nights chords of redemption.

I fumbled with excuses about the storm. The more he lingered, the more confused I became until I finally grabbed my pack in a flurry, convincing him it was only his errands that were taking me away.

I cried all the way to town as the road wound treacherously around the cliffs of the canyon. Gary's truck felt like a disoriented lone craft caught in the gravitational pull of a runaway galaxy. The storm must have been fleeting. This side of the canyon was still cheery with early afternoon sunshine. I clutched the wheel, wet with my tears, as the two-lane road abruptly divided into a four-lane highway. Then it opened onto a straightaway, with a mirage, posing as a never-ending pool of liquid nourishment streaming down the center of the open road. It was only an illusion, I heard the voice within me say, like Gary's love.

His Ford lurched and came to a halt in front of the general store where he told me I would find grain for the animals and basic supplies for us. Just as he had said, crowds of spick and span tourists gawked at pricey art and new age paraphernalia on the turn of the century sidewalks lined with shops. The grainery was stacked with barrels of bulk grains, nuts, granola and loose-leaf teas. Two children left their mother's side and wandered to the back where canaries, desert iguanas, Mexican parrots and a basket of pedigree albino pups were hidden behind bushels of wild oats.

As I priced the bulgur and mixed corn for Gary's rooster, one of two small boys lifted the latch off the guinea pig's cage. The pigs let out a squeal as I grabbed one of the boys to my chest. His tender energy filled me with sweetness as my face soured. I could barely restrain myself, feeling scales on my back rise, and the skin on my skull grow taught, while my eyes darted. The Wastress commanded me with her reptilian hunger. Repulsed, I grabbed the cornered pig. The shopkeeper tapped me on the shoulder.

"Thank you" He said. "That would have been the third guinea pig this week. I wish she'd just once keep her eyes on these brats, but I haven't seen a parent discipline a child here in the last twenty years. They don't want to damage their spirits." He shook his head and walked away. I was shaking with horror. I wanted that child for something too horrible to know. Fighting the impulse to take the boy with me, I set him down, making my way to the cashier.

Hysterical, I couldn't start Gary's Ford. When I looked out the windshield sand was blowing in fits of spiraling dust and debris, packing his dented hood like a burial mound. I feared the fuel pump would be impacted with sand but, somehow, the old truck turned over. Slamming on the accelerator, I scarcely missed the crosswalk brimming with running tourists. The sandstorm pelted my face and eyes, pushing in through the sun-cracked rubber gaps of the old chassis. Rage consumed the valley.

I don't know how I maneuvered his truck to stay on the road. I could hardly see all the way back to his casita. Clouds of dust and tears assaulted me while rage tore at me from inside. When I opened Gary's door he was by the stove bating a blaze that was rising up his kitchen wall.

"Damn it, the whole things burnt," he cried. "I wanted to surprise you with Mostacolli." He said, in tears. Then, without another word or acknowledgment he swung open the door and raced outside. Standing alone in his burning kitchen, like a sand caste of a raging Aphrodite I watched dumbly as the smoke mushroomed around me.

Chapter

20

As the flames scaled up Gary's kitchen wall I searched for something to quell them. In a panic I threw the water jar at his flaming Tibetan calendar. It coiled like an angry mother snake spitting flames at my feet. Then the kitchen drapes caught fire. I knocked them behind the stove with his broom. Throwing open the door, it was impossible to see more than a few inches in front of me. I felt my Wastress jaw, huge and reptilian, fill with sand, but my calls for help were muted by the desert's wrath.

"Gary please, I don't know what to do. Where is the switch to turn off the propane?" I called futilely as the sand unleashed a siren's wailing blast. It smarted my skin, like bullets driving me back into his house. The casita was on fire. I found the spigot for his hose when another blast shook every movable object. I reeled as his cow heads and snakeskins flew at me. Then I heard the hot tub outside buckle like a god cracking his knuckles. Pillows and beads, towels and underwear, guitar picks, kitchen wear and candles all attacked me like a militia commanded by the brigadier wind.

As I lost consciousness the portal took me with an urgency that overcame all concerns for my physical fate. I hungered more for truth than survival. I wanted to be with her, to solve the mystery that we shared.

"Please help me, help me to free myself of this Wastress madness. Take me back if you must" I pleaded searching for the entrance into her world. Then, in a blast of cold air, I could feel her icy hand pulling me and I let go to her aid.

"I'll help you, I'll do whatever it takes, but tell me queen of Egypt, how can we break this curse when you hold the key and you are lost to your own madness?" In total darkness she began to whisper "Our madness may trap you, even after I show you, beware. It is one thieving deep shadow hidden where no one dares look, more powerful as it attaches itself to what we fear and to what we are most fond of. There are no guarantees knowing the truth will free you. The deep shadow has ruled silently in our denial tumbling down generations, let loose always tragically, always perfectly timed to destroy love. Be my scribe if you like, dear doctor of modern psychology, but beware. You will not find your answers with the part of your mind you are so comfortable toting as reality. Not until every hideous invisible motive reaches the light of consciousness will you be free. We women could, if we would hold together through the lies, through the denial. We are the ones to alter the story. Come, I need you now. Help me to face it head on. But be advised, I will fight you in every way.

Ask your questions, doctor."

"What was the turning point that set your cool rage ablaze into this uncontrolled madness we share? Why did you let your husband exchange your daughter's hearts for chaos? For what reason would a mother place her daughter's fate on her man's chopping block?"

"Understand me", she moaned "dear scribe, please find the trip-switch in your heart to end this."

Stealing the Moon

Act II

Scene 2

[Wind whips Nefertiti as she makes her way down a corridor of blowing panels. I fear I have brought my storm to her.]

Nefertiti: No, he has brought his storm to seduce you. And still your denial weakens you. You cannot resist him. May your knowledge through me one day make you strong enough to chose differently. I will give you all I have, but I too will weaken. Then I will need you to pull me out. You have come back to witness how I became bound. It is our bargain sister, our addiction to warm ourselves cooking on coals of hatred. Scribe, doctor, here is our day.

[Anger beats the wind swept corridor. Gradually it becomes clear there is another force that blows the panels. It is the echoing pleas of a lovesick pharaoh. Queen Nefertiti watches cloaked behind the blowing panels as her husband lies on his obsidian bed with his handsome young lover, and cousin, Smenkhkare.]

Smenkhkara: You cannot hold me to you with lies, Akenhaten. All Egypt knows I can never replace your beloved Queen Nefertiti.

Akenhaten: Even if she no longer suits my needs?

Smenkhkara: What needs could the great priest of the Aten

possibly still possess? Come Pharaoh, does not your god fill your every desire with his daily fire?

Akenhaten: Yes, except in this one regard. Do not make me speak against Egypt's queen to keep you by my side. Must I say it aloud, Smenkhkara? Very well, this wounded body hungers only for your manly touch. What more must I declare to assure you? Do you think because she has always been by my side another cannot overtake my heart? A good watchdog remains loyal to her master but only to keep usurpers at bay. Egypt sees Nefertiti as their defender, as their love. But for me. No. It has not been so since your return from the north. How much longer must I pretend when she is no more to me than any older sister bound by duties obligation.

Smenhkhara: Nefertiti captivates all Egypt with her cat eyes carved above every doorway. Look outside your window. Amarna waits to bask in her regal beauty. You cannot expect me to believe that I will ever be immortalized, with equal stature. I am no fool.

Akenhaten: Do not be so quick to dismiss how I shall render you to greet future men. Your finely carved image will grace our temple's walls. Let historians postulate over the bond between us, I do not care. [Smenkhkara throws his head up and struts for the door, unbelieving.]

Akenhaten: [Pulling Smenhkhara back, the pharaoh rips open his gown.] This belongs only to you! Do not leave me cousin. Shuffling skirts will never draw this magnet. My daughters are my obligation to the divine. Soon you will hear all Egypt at your door begging for your audience. Nefertiti thinks she commands the winds that kite my heartstrings but they are tied only to you dear cousin. [The two men embrace]

Nefertiti: Ahhh, here it is now, scribe. Look deep into the face of desire there in my strongest need he copulates. [She falls spreading her legs, laughing wildly.}

Natalie: Stop, stop this queen. Once you were a great woman.

[Nefertiti grabs my hair and makes me watch]

Smenkhkara: [kissing Akenhaten caressing his loins] Queen Nefertiti cannot be so lightly dismissed, she is legend. A woman loved for her own determination. They see her, and your daughters as the mother's way to temper your hot hierophant's tongue.

Akenhaten: [rubbing his lovers legs and buttock] The way of the mother? What fool will believe in her after we have delivered Egypt into this glorious renaissance? Nefertiti has birthed me seven stars to fuel my revolution. For this she will always have compensation. But I cannot quiet what yearns for your touch. [The two begin to make love] Egypt's queen has lost me. I cannot fight this.

Smenkhkara: She carries a great star's fire, for that she remains their adored icon. [Pushing away an aroused pharaoh] How can I be sure you do not say all this just to keep me closeted by your side, for play?

Akenhaten: [fully erect with desire] She does not cause me to wake panting for her touch as you do, cousin. My mind does not sooth while dreaming of her body's comfort. I have no hunger left for Queen Nefertiti.

[Holding her belly Queen Nefertiti wails as though someone had cut out a piece of her. I try to comfort her but she pushes me aside.]

Nefertiti: Do not attempt to comfort a queen whose husband rams their divine destiny up the anus of his cousin for all Egypt to see. What anecdote do you possess for this humiliation? What say you that could draw up reassurance now? Read me from the book of the dead? There is not light enough in all of Egypt to resurrect this queen. She is left to ride the edge of dead space, a mad women, unwilling to live with such pain, while adultery masquerades as holiness. We came to birth a sacred light together to ease suffering through our love's uniting. I am lost, scattered to his fornicating wind. My soul's mission cannot be accomplished without our polarities uniting. I am hope's broken arm left dangling, without the blood to grow new marrow. How long can I lay here left for dead, bleeding in this cavity where he has bludgeoned my name? As he plows into his boy, so am I satiated with hatred's madness. I prefer to be crazed rather than endure this my public execution.

Come revenge be my cure! Help me to withstand the stench of this carcass, our holy union slaughtered! His seed, so squandered, has become the ink to blacken the record of my life. Husband, think this out again. I am the needle that pricks until there is no more blood left to make you erect. Let your God try to find a remedy for me!

Scene 3

Nefertiti: Months pass, my husband, Egypt's darling, keeps his sex temple afloat, without opposition, quietly letting rumors spread that I have become gravely ill.

[Enter a disenfranchised priest of the old order now appearing to be one of Akenhaten's allies.]

Calsiturn: Forgive me queen. He will not stop with your daughter's in his bed. He intends to marry one after the other, but first he must put you to pasture. He has signed the documents that determine you too ill to coregent Egypt. He has made you a palace tower, fitting an aging queen, where you can meditate and grow your wisdom in solitude.

Nefertiti: You who lift your pharaoh onto his own daughter's womb would follow such a decree?

Calsiturn: What am I to do my lady, he holds Egypt hostage.

Nefertiti: Then lock me in his madwoman's palace tower, prisoner of the war between us. Shield me from the stench of his adultery and incest. I wish no further ownership in his history. Bring me to his jail. Come tomorrow and I shall join your conspiracy. I know all you need to freeze him from his mummy forever. His immortality ends with me. He will not pillage the soul of woman without consequence.

[Calsiturn reluctantly calls for his men to take her away]

Nefertiti: Surely you know his god must be a voyeur perverse as his servant. Or does his all seeing eye go blind while the rapist priest takes his own daughters to his bed? How does he now take each of my little girls? Do you watch? Does he persuade them god would agree that his rod is divine and to sex him is to have them know their heavenly father? Rise up with me against the monster, let the world judge him as Inanna would. She, Goddess from whom all becoming arises, the mistress of heaven and the house of life, mistress of the word of god, she wisest of all magicians, let justice rule! Destroy the mad-sexed dog that raped the goddess out of each of my little girls lovely set of thighs. Do it.

Las Madrinas County Hospital. Three days later

"Kill his immortal dream and save Egypt from his curse." I moaned as two nurses loosened the straps that tied me to my bed.

167

As they rotated me, I shrieked with pain, engulfed in present time memories of the fire at Gary's casita.

"Is this the burn unit?" I asked of the masked nurse changing my bandages.

"No. You have no burns."

"No burns?"

"You were brought here because of the explosion."

"Explosion? How could I have escaped without burns?" I whispered, weak from my injuries. "The house wasn't on fire?" The nurses looked at each other in bewilderment, as I fought to surface my awareness.

They read from the police report. It sounded like mumbles spoken across an empty stadium as they continued to swab iodine onto the dozens of stinging holes that lined my back.

"Doctor Stearn sustained multiple lacerations resulting from the windows imploding during last weeks storm." I opened my eyes, certain my last recollection was being abandoned as Gary fled his burning house.

"Hundreds of glass particles were pulled out of her back, arms and shoulders. Most of them could be removed but not all.

"Gary?" I moaned

"He's alright. Do you want to see him?" One of the uniformed women asked straightening the pale curtains that scarcely shielded my wounds from the scorching rays of the Arizona sun.

"He's here?"

"Yes. He's here and without a scratch on him."

Drifting in and out of consciousness I remembered the warnings "His instability will only weaken you." I was sure what raged through my mind was a lie, certain he had done his best trying to help me. Then my mind raved again. Why didn't he have one laceration?

Shaking, unable to speak, Gary just sat there strumming his guitar all afternoon by my hospital bed. In dreams I rode the tides of Nefertit's mad hatred as his notes wore me down. I could not rest with him by my side. When he broke a string I hoped he would stop, but he kept repeating that same hideous song.

I was livid with self-righteous contempt, suddenly certain Gary was nothing but a set up, a schizophrenic crazed lyricist unable to complete even a single song. The stacks of unfinished songs thrown on his bedroom floor flooded my mind. He was completely non-functional. Why else would he have left me in his burning house?

"Get out of here, just leave me alone." I screamed, my teeth clenched.

"You shouldn't have left us." He mumbled, "That morning, if you had just stayed with me, none of this would have happened, don't you see?"

I was enraged that he was blaming me. I was covered in shrapnel because he had left me alone to extinguish a fire that he had started.

"I'd prefer the cobra, just like you Gary. Remember, 'at least you know when he's threatening your life' didn't you say that? I'd rather be with a man who let me know up front he'd rather bolt than live in this revolving madhouse with you. It was you who left me for dead in your casita. I want to believe in you I do. But it's impossible. You don't have the strength to help me with this. It's not fair to pretend you do, then run out the door when it gets too rough. Just leave me alone." I cried grabbing for my pillow.

I never thought the sight of Abe Levi would be anything but a sorry one. I was mistaken.

"Natalie, I've been half way around this canyon with the search and rescue team. What the hell happened to you? Don't you know better than to go sight seeing when a sand storm alert is posted?" Abe embraced me with one of his papa bear hugs. Resting in his arms brought me my first moment of comfort since the fire.

"How did you know where to find me?" I asked, smiling at the worry in his deep-set eyes.

"When you never returned any of my messages I asked around. Miriam, the bus driver told me she had left you out at the ruins.

169

How could you go there? Aren't you here to heal? That was the most dangerous place to be."

"Why?"

"Because that's where the sand storm turned into a twister."

He held me in his arms and I must have fallen asleep. When I awoke Gary was at our knees.

He mumbled some phrase inaudibly over and over again like a nun repeats her Hail Mary's until I screamed.

"Get out, just get out and don't ever come back, not ever, do you hear?"

Chapter

21

The Shambhala Lodge, One week later

Shambhala was lit like a Renaissance Cathedral the night of my return. Charlotte and Janis helped me across the solarium pointing out the golden, foot long, crystal lanterns they lit each night praying for my healing. Hundreds of candle flames illumined Yogicar's disciples adorned in celebrational gemstones of jade, opal, ruby and diamond. Their countenances wrapped in glimmering turbans hung motionless, changing masks that flickered hidden between layered personas. A surge of emotion flooded me with images of Jesus condemned to death, while Jerusalem feasted and danced. I could make no sense of it nor could I shake my feelings of enormous sorrow. As we made our way to the elevators, a welcoming line of Yogicar's women reached out their hands to congratulate me on my good fortune. A companion of Janis and Charlotte draped in an orange sarong whispered, "We were so grateful you survived the blast. Would it be possible to meet with you when you are fully recovered? We think what happened to you is a miracle."

"You mean that I wasn't burned to a crisp?" I retorted.

"No, that your friend was able to put out that blaze before the big blast hit. Miriam said there really wasn't time, but it all worked out," as she spoke her smile widened, expecting a show of gratitude in return.

"What are you talking about? Gary ran out on me. He left me alone in his burning house. I still don't understand how I wasn't burned alive in that blast."

"Didn't he tell you? Haven't you spoken? You must have lost consciousness. He put out the fire. Miriam cornered him. She got him to tell her everything. Gary ran out to get his high-pressure hose. He had to run, fetch it from his shed. He felt terrible leaving you but he had to get in and out in a hurry to seal the doorway from the storm. It was a huge funnel. When he didn't get back in time to protect you from the twister, he felt so terrible he just went autistic or something, but Miriam shook him out of it. The explosion must have shocked your memory. If he hadn't put out that fire you wouldn't be alive." As Charlotte helped me into the glass elevator then down the hall to my room what she was telling me quacked with another inner explosion. I crumbled to my knees sobbing in remorse, like a zombie awakening from a trance. Her words broke my spell. I wanted to see Gary, to laugh like children with him again in his garden of herbs, to relax, make love, to have another day with him, this time making wiser choices. I had misinterpreted him completely and I missed him terribly. Pulling myself together I vowed silently to wait until the journey with Nefertiti was resolved. I would never bring him in to it again, not after what I had already done.

Unlocking my door, Charlotte went on to explain why I had become an instant celebrity at Shambhala. She and Janis had told the others about the psychologist with the love goddess friend. They all wanted to hear <u>Shemura and Her Men.</u> Yogicar had pushed them too far, asking that they annul their marriage vows the night before the festival of light ended. He had a revelation, that married life would only undermine their effectiveness to serve God. They were beginning to realize he meant only to serve himself at their cost. They were waiting for my return, hoping I might captain their mutiny.

In the days that followed I read <u>Shemura and Her Men</u> to enclaves of Yogicar's defunct brides and their befuddled husbands. In between I starred at the desert tundra, numb to the full extent of my betrayal. Gary had not abandoned me at all. He had saved my life! By Saturday late afternoon the last of them had wandered off. It was then I was shaken with a third explosion. Her laughter tore through me.

"It's the misery we love isn't it Natalie?" The Wastress taunted.

"No" I fired back. I was determined that this was not going to be her triumph. I made plans to return to Gary's casita the next day. It did not matter if he ever talked to me again. At least I could apologize, help him to heal from the damage I had created. I imagined him with his apron on, cooking for me, smiling, kissing my neck. I felt the crescendo of my female spirit tenderly loved as his Mary Magdalene. What took me so far away? How could I so easily relinquish this young man's love that was helping me restore myself to life? It was a mistake, one that caused him incredible pain, but not an irredeemable one. I vowed to overturn her victory, to go to him as soon as the next bus ran out to the pyramids.

Just then Janis and Charlotte pounded on my door. Janis rushed into my living room, wailing, "Natalie, we are so very sorry, but there's nothing anyone could have done. He had a history of mental illness. Everyone knew that. No one knew until it was too late." They were both shrieking with grief. "It was so sad, Miriam said he looked just like Jesus, everyone got off the bus and just wept, people that didn't even know him. Miriam said in all her years it was the strangest thing she had ever witnessed at Las Madrinas."

Las Madrinas Chapel of the last Good-bye, three days later

Gary would have been self-conscious with the unnaturalness of his funeral. It was an empty ceremony preformed by people who didn't really know him. Miriam's sister pumped out 'Amazing Grace' on the old church organ for the room packed with acquaintances. Janis and Charlotte, a few canyon characters, Miriam and myself were the only people who had been touched by his presence. Not even his family showed up. His mother didn't have the heart to tell her Italian clan that her oldest son Gary had hung himself, on a cross, in the desert, just like their beloved savior, Jesus. Cousins and distant nephews, at a loss for what to do, pitched in on a garish Vegas-style bouquet of plastic roses to circumfuse his ashes. I couldn't believe that such rare passion was now ash in this vase. The vase looked like it was bought off the discard bin at Woolworth's. Two spiders sauntered across Gary's picture, then disappeared behind a pair of porcelain Angels starring upwards with a painted on pomposity. As I mourned, the rage that seduced me from him sat in silent victory. I had let myself become the accomplice to his murder. Now nothing I could do would end his mockery.

I visited his house one last time in the rain that lingered following the freak storm. His casita was a drizzle soaked rubble. His song sheets were stuck to the downed chicken wire fencing. I peeled one off and sang it to his animals that were loose and wandering, frightened and hungry. Gradually they made a circle around me and stared me down, looking at me with what I would not accept. Gary had committed suicide. I was, in a very direct way responsible and I would never see him again. I had lost the tender beginnings of love given to me from a man who would have gladly torn a piece of his jagged heart out to lend me strength. I, who dreamed of transforming into a resurrected warrior of light, had treated him with the heartlessness of a Judas.

My shoes were caked with mud and debris. The whole place was junked, totally destroyed. Walking his yard, I gathered up more sheets of withered lyrics. I felt like a murderess removing evidence from her own crime scene. Then, I was interrupted, by chanting. I looked up across the desert, reverberating from avalanches of moisture to see the peaks of five hooded men disappearing into the pyramid. He had been telling the truth all along, the truth about everything!

All day I walked the muddied desert floor, crying with the deep pain of awakening too late to my complicity. I slide under his tarp, opened the Ford, found an old crayon in his glove compartment and wrote my eulogy. When it was finished, I pulled the tarp back, walked to the pyramid then scaled its steps. From the top, chaos gloated like a gleeful vulture encircling his death scene. Gary's cross swayed with his hanged man's noose in the saturated wind. It played with his memory, like a spiteful child tears apart her favorite doll, then feeds its dismembered appendages to the draft. Tantrums of rain and sand vied with me as I read. I prayed for him to know he did not leave this world as he had most feared, completely incomprehensible.

"Gary," I read from the altar-top, "I helped tattoo you to the arm of power, a side-show Jesus welded to my turncoat heart. You were a new kind of man, come to topple the old world tower built by the cowards of deceit. You were armed only with the passion to love, helping me to retrieve what I had sold them for protection. Now all that is left are spiders crawling in and out of your five and dime shrine. They cannot diminish the all or nothing man you were. I cowered at the hard-way-bingo of your truth delivered through the fluctuations of your pain. It was I who ran from our burning house, a coward myself, no better than Abe, slithering away from the dedication it takes to bring anyone back to love. What do the spiders seek, crawling on your dead rose bouquet? What is there left to feed upon?"

"Natalie, the bridge created by even a day of genuine connection is so rich the velvet legged ladies cannot resist. Listen, we may not have long." Gary's voice came to me through the wetness of rain and sorrow. As he spoke the pain I had sent through his heart pierced mine like a knife. I held my chest, this time refusing to cower as the monks began a fresh round of chanting.

"Gary? How can I hear you? Is this just another one of my mind games?"

"No, Natalie, it is me, really, the only person who has ever seen your Wastress first hand. Her energy is what you see out there now, spitting fits where I took my life. Please, there is no time for proof. I am only given a short time to come through. If you are sincere about wanting to set things right, there may be something you can still do."

"Why would you want to help me now?" I asked.

"We are both abusers of life's gifts and opportunities. Taking my life was as blind as your contempt for me. But it's not all ours. Huge fields of energy thrown at us to stop loves return manipulate us. It's been that way for a very long time. I'm not in hell for what I did, well, that's not exactly true, I am. Even so, I have been shown more love here than I ever believed could exist and if your willing, I could be free of this place and go on, soon. Are you Natalie? Can you still hear me?"

"Yes, Oh yes, I hear you like a mama dolphin hears her strayed baby. Sonar ears, perfect, yes. I'll do anything, tell me what can I do to help you?"

"I'm kinda lucky, in a weird way. Not in our cruelty but because I got caught in more energy than I could handle. I'm being given a kind of deal. We've both let ourselves succumb to our own fatal errors. But, here love and mercy are the stronger considerations. They have shown me you might be able to hear me, and if you did, you might listen. We can work together to end this. You can't go on with Akenhaten using you like he does, to carry on his campaign against love and I need to get out of here, even if the next little while is a non-stop roller coaster of torturous revelations. I'm willing if you are." His voice faded as I struggled to hear.

"I'm in a huge hellish cavern. But its not hell, it's a real place hidden somewhere in the collective unconscious energy matrix. There are many children here. Not exactly children, just a part of their essence, a piece of their soul's energy force, do you understand? They all have one thing in common. They died, abandoned in horrible shock and great pain, then they were taken here to be trapped forever in their final moments of hopelessness. It's too atrocious to fathom, but its real. They're prisoners and they're not isolated cases, a lot of souls are kept in places like this, I have seen them. I only know part of their story. Does this make any sense? There are lots of ways of ripping off people's soul force; war, poverty, disease, disaster, creating the illusion of world scarcity to foster ceaseless horror scenes of desecration. We can't forget greed, nor how it hides in all the skewed media information that insulates society from knowing the external manipulations for world dominance. On the surface, power is making a genocide of the third world and is pillaging the middle class, while creating an ever-widening chasm between rich and poor. But where I am, this is a whole other aspect of abusive power. This is what is happening inside the collective energy in our own unconscious.

"Why can't all the love you said was with you there release the orphaned children?" I asked him.

"Because it is humanities time to awaken. It is our time to take responsibility for what we have collectively allowed. Our collective complicity created this and only we can end it. Will you finish the play Natalie, return to Egypt one last time? I have been shown Nefertiti has the truth and can expose the dynamics of how this actually works. As people listen, and begin to wake up to what's really happening they will start to release powers invisible hold on humanity. That will help the souls caught here. This is horrific, Natalie. The traumatized energies of babies who died in orphanages and hospitals, on battlefields and in disasters are trapped here. Their souls are being captured, and tortured here on the other side. It's like the worst imaginable sci-fi horror movie, but its real."

"It is not fair that you are trapped with them, Gary. You tried to get me through, you were just too weak and too hurt to sustain your love. It wasn't your fault, not even your death. I should have helped you grow stronger instead I lent strength to your weakness."

"That's all true but taking my own life has its own set of consequences. We are all responsible to heal our relationship with life. You did lend strength to my hopelessness but blaming only makes things worse. Natalie what I am about to tell you, you may not want to hear."

I pleaded for him to go on.

"When I left you with Abe in the hospital I felt you, like a murderess, entering me through my vulnerability with a whipping relentless wind, overcoming my emotions with hopelessness. At first I tried to fight you but in the end I gave in. I could hear the priests the whole time. The Wastress is a killer and somehow she is a part of you.

If you are sincere you will return one last time to Egypt. I can't stay much longer. Pray. Use everything you know. I will be with you. You'll have the earth's protection if you can find a cave called the 'Cave of the Womb.' Get Nefertiti to relive the truth no matter how it goes against the popular notions of their history. Transcribe what you experience and perform it for the world to see." As he spoke his voice broke up like a cell phone going out of range.

"What good would that do?" I called out trying to pull him back.

"Natalie the place where I must now exist is like a blood sea storming with the terrorized wails of dead women and children. You have the memory." He responded straining to stay with me.

"What if it doesn't work, if the current world won't accept this? They're not likely to want our story told." I shouted feeling him floating far from me.

"The earth will find others to seed the future, not with fear or hate or selfishness. Now is the end for all that. You decide. I can come through one last time in the 'Cave of the Womb.' If you are a tool for destruction you can become an instrument for creation."

Chapter

22

I opened my blouse to the late afternoon sun. It was burning my chest, like iodine trying to disinfect the septic heart I shared with Nefertiti. Desperately I clung to my communion with Gary but there was only the sound of the pyramid purring like a satisfied cat ignoring me. Its self-satisfied hum pushed me down the craggy incline. With each step I resolved to do everything Gary had asked of me. I could feel Nefertiti weeping, confirming Akenhaten's predatory nature still thrived inside both of us, that we had not uncovered enough truth to dislodge his hold. As I made my way back, in one pathetic moment the wind played with Gary's hanging noose, slapping my face in victory.

As I arrived at the temple's base, Charlotte and Janis ran to greet me, waving their arms like two buttercup dervishes twirling in the untamed sage.

"We hope you don't mind that we've come looking for you. It's really a terrible time, we know, it's just that everyone else is so caught up with Yogicar. We have to get away. We're ready to cleanse ourselves of all his brainwashing. Oh, this is really bad timing. We'll just go. We're so sorry."

"No, stay, please," I pleaded, grateful for their comradery.

"We wish we could have known a true avatar like Krishnamurti or Shemura, not a hypocrite like Yogicar. But even knowing what's real, it's difficult to stand up when everyone we know still believes in him. We could use a little…support." They blushed while pulling two carved statues from their pack.

"I don't wish any disrespect to Gary. We just had to do something different. We were up all night, inspired." Charlotte declared her green eyes brilliant with fresh intensity. "These are just like the ones the priestesses used as magical talismans to link their prayers to the power of the Great Mother Goddess," Charlotte pronounced. "We've been reading past curfew," Still blushing she displayed her book entitled The Once and Future Goddess."

"Women made temples like wombs in the earth, for prayer and mediation. They were just big enough to cradle the priestesses bodies." Janis stopped as she spotted my blouse, soaked with tears and my eyes still swollen with grief and torment.

"Here," she said handing me one of the two full-breasted figurines. I had the impulse to give the primordial forms back, fearing to keep them would just be more thieving from innocents. But as I held them to my heart their deep magic shattered my pretense. It was time to tell them about Gary and what had transpired, to reveal almost everything, including my encounters with Nefertiti. As I concluded, their bird goddess carvings began to shake in my hands, like a divining rod, until my vibrating hands pointed at my copy of the play, Stealing the Moon. The young women gasped, holding onto each other.

"That's it! Perform the play, for everyone!" You could break Akenhaten's curse and shatter Yogicar's hold. Stage Stealing the Moon at Shambhala Lodge. Why not?"

"That's Gary's vision as well. But, I'm not sure, I don't know how it ends. The last scene is missing, the crucial one where Nefertiti reveals the mechanism of her madness, and mine. I have to return one last time. But I'm not sure I can."

"With all that has happened to you, here surely you must believe you'll discover what you need to know." They shamed my two faces with their newfound nerve. I watched as an ultraviolet halo formed around the two young women, portending their future. Would they transform themselves and redefine their spirituality as two modern neophyte priestesses of the moon?

"Have either of you ever heard of a place called the 'Cave of the Womb?' I need to find it before nightfall."

"I've heard of it but never actually gone there." Janis replied. "Women have come from all over just to do ceremony there. It's legend that Native American Indian women gave birth inside. But the local tribal elders claim it's much older than even their history. How did you hear about it?"

"From Gary." I said.

"That's incredible! You really never heard of it before?" Charlotte questioned, her mouth falling open with appreciation for Gary's invisible support.

"No, never." I replied.

"How miraculous that Gary is reaching to you wanting to help, even now. Maybe he's right, in the 'Cave of the Womb' Akenhaten wouldn't be able to hide his secrets anymore. The Earth will help us expose Yogicar and Akenhaten at the same time. What's the difference between them? They both make the same kind of trouble, it's just that one is in a body, at the moment. If you like we can go back to the lodge for supplies and research the directions for the cave. Do you want to come with us or are you going to stay out here on your own?" Charlotte asked.

"I have to stay. I can't go back until I keep my promise to Gary and Shemura."

"You promised Shemura something?" Janis asked shooting me a weary glance.

"Yes, I promised to persist until my female spirit began to re-direct my life." The words moved like a haunting through my throat.

"What will that take?" Charlotte asked earnestly.

"Discovering what women like me did to become mad with destructive power. There is one thing more. I'm going to need someone to keep watch, while I'm out."

As we embraced they promised to help, returning before nightfall with supplies and my transcription equipment. I waited out the afternoon pacing Gary's yard. As I fed his animals, I was sure I heard the cries of the women and children wailing coming through Gary's pleas, aching for release. Dusk made a serape of fuchsia and gold in the twilight sky when Yogicar's jeep landed, covering me with dirt and laughter. The raven squawked in recognition. The tumbleweed twins were back, pleased with themselves. Waving a piece of paper and pulling three beers and a bottle of Madeira out of their pack, they popped open the cans and handed me the bottle.

"We told Yogicar we couldn't make it to his Sat Sang tonight. 'Sorry old boy got to go help the lady doctor clean up Gary's casita.' Didn't mention Gary was assisting you, from 'the other side', in getting the old guru's sorry ass exposed."

"How about a little female merriment?" Janis said smiling through her tears. "The bastard told me I was going to birth the Son of God with him. I'm such a lonely sucker. I spent the last month sneaking into his bed every morning. It's time to celebrate our break-up doc. Look," she sobbed, her laughter sending crying streams down her arms, blotting a paper she held tightly. Treasure hunt solved. Dana, our housemother, knows all about the 'Cave of the Womb.' She had stories to fill the afternoon, stories of children born up there. Their sweetness is legend and so are their special gifts. Some grew to be seers or geniuses, others became major artists standing in the strength of their spirit, no matter what. She told us the elders suspect the cave's healing reputation began even earlier. Prehistoric ancient priestesses performed their magic rituals inside. Charlotte's laughter broke open into a full grin, exposing two chipped teeth. "Your not the only gang rape victim in the camp, but never mind, it's time for action right?" she yelped "Freedom" over and over until the canyon shook with outrage and fresh daring. Janis proudly handed me the map lit by her neon pink flashlight.

"Come on, let's stand up for once doc," Charlotte shouted, handing me another almost emptied bottle of Madeira.

Yogicar's jeep blasted into the navy blue twilight, rocking us with live performance from Las Madrina's Equinox Gala. We skid along the canyon's cliffs like three runaway slaves until the vulva of the 'Cave of the Womb' spread unashamed across the sunset cliffs, sending our screeching buggy to a sudden halt. Two clearly etched burgundy lips waited high upon the canyon's far wall.

"Welcome doctor of contemporary madness. Before you lie the ancient secrets of the great silenced mother. Abandon all bullshit, yea, who shimmy up her thigh" Janis pronounced, refusing to be put off by the tears that continued to redden her already flushed face. We were flexed and ready, standing across from the entrance to the 'Cave of the Womb.'

An hour's hike is all it'll take" Janis calculated.

"How am I going to scale that rock wall before dark?" I asked.

"Tow rope rescue!" Charlotte yelped. She was whipping a cord of hemp, lariat style, into the crisp high desert air from the back of Yogicar's Jeep." I spent my summers with the cowboy part of my family. Here, try on my boots. Don't want you using another rattler as an excuse to scoot out of what you got to do." Charlotte handed me her spare pair of brown hiking boots. As twilight stilled the creatures of the desert we made our private prayers gazing upward at the towering rock vagina. Then we marched breathing in the intoxication of desert flowers bursting with rare potency, released by the freak desert storm. By the time we made our way to the canyon's distant wall, my feet had swollen and were throbbing. I remembered Gary. "No one believes it except crazy people and the Indians but the Earth is conscious, just like you or me."

Then Janis took a swig of Madeira and shouted," Come on doc, get your butt up to the mama's womb."

"Yeah don't make us wait much longer. This is it. Don't make us think you're just a female version of Yogicar," Charlotte shouted. And Janis jumped on board "I'm done with this, I am so done with this," she yelled exposing her broken grin to the last rays of daylight. "Don't cop out or we ain't coming back to get ya." Charlotte slurred, boldly.

"Yeah, get it straight this time or we may not even come back at all." I shuddered sensing the burgeoning justice beginning to form in the minds of the world's victims of power, soon to comprehend what has been done to them without their knowing.

As they chanted, "You better do it." They lassoed the cedar pine quarter way up. I made my first few attempts up the wall, unsuccessfully. Finally, balancing the pain in my foot with the importance of my mission, I held my position, securing my feet at the entrance.

They hoisted my supplies up the sandy ledge after me. As I acclimated inside to the cool damp earthen womb shaped interior, I shivered with what I might have to face. Hurrying to organize my camp before total darkness set in, I placed my sleeping bag on the circular earthen floor then arranged my recording equipment, food, water and flashlight all within an arm's reach.

The last feathers of sunlight danced, stroking the massive lips, then disappeared. The air was creamy and rich with the promise of rebirth. Darkness clothed the cave like the touch of a black furry coat. I followed my remote viewing protocol, dreaming and waking and dreaming again, feeling I was being held in life's womb of transformation, the void before all creation.

A tension hovered like a mother bear sitting, concealed in a hidden corner, alert but silent. All night long I practicing my techniques and prayed but neither voices nor visions come. By morning I had recorded nothing. I was empty of the voyage.

Charlotte and Janis climbed the hemp ladder to bring me fresh food and water then shimmied out of sight without a word, as we had agreed upon. The second night fireflies light the electric air. My nerves jumped from sounds I imagined coming from rattlers or scorpions, ready to strike at my belly. I couldn't sleep and still there were no visions. By the third night, my mind raced with exhaustion and fear. I was sure I had come all this way for nothing more than to be eaten by a mother mountain bear at the end of her patience. Trembling, I imagined her hungry breath impregnating the thick night air. Then I remembered Gary saying he could come through one last time if I needed him.

"Gary, if you can hear me I do need your help now. I've used all my remote viewing skills. This has never happened before. Las Madrinas has been a non-stop assault of phenomena up until now. Why can't I see or hear anything?"

"Be patient. The Earth is helping you build the force to break your resistance. It takes time." I heard him say.

By the fourth day a fierce battle raged inside my body. Familiar obsessions pounded at me, hungering to be satisfied, still I could see nothing.

"Take the talismans and hold them to your heart, especially the one with the golden wings." I heard Gary say.

I had not noticed that one of the hand sized statues had painted wings but, as my eyes strained with the help of the moon's light I saw her and remembered Nefertiti's affinity with the Egyptian bird goddess before she let herself fall under the spell of the Aten. I held it tightly, remembering Shemura's and Ruby's words. The Earth is alive, speaking, it was time to listen. Gary's voice repeated, "She's actually helping you to build the life force within yourself to overcome the energetic mistakes of the past."

The tiny statue pulsed as I held it to my heart. Gary whispered, "Now pray."

"Mother of all life help me to break the bonds that tie me to this pharaoh's demolition of the feminine psyche, this curse of the mind, this urge to destroy life, going against all that is sacred compassionate and truly feminine. Let me know what must be done in order to end this and heal my relationship with life."

Before me appeared a majestic cobalt blue phoenix with flame red feathers framing it's breast of gold. The giant bird held in her mouth the babe I had been forty years earlier. I watched as she set my little body before me on fire. Then she dropped my ashes carelessly and flew away. I heard my baby wails but could do nothing to save myself. I cried out to Gary in disbelief,

"This is the Great Mother's healing for me? To burn me, as an innocent child, before my eyes?"

Then the mythological bird flew back, landing on my chest and spoke. "Yes, daughter of tarnished light. The Mother gives you this chance to become human. But first there must be justice. You are now one with all the victims of power, one with Gary and the orphaned entrapped homeless women and children, with your daughter and the daughter's of Nefertiti, great souls whose light have been violated. Your fate unites with the many whose attempt to humanize mankind has been slowed, thieved through deception. Millions still drift now, without anchor in the whirlpool of poverty, disease, oppression and psychic torment. Today as you lay here praying to restore your lost spirit, old plots and agendas wave victory flags across the globe. The cover up of truth goes on and on as power consolidates, casting its net of suppression and misery. The energies of humanity at this very moment are still being held hostage. This is what war and fear serve. Align your prayers with the prayers of the Divine Mother. You are a part of her. The change in world consciousness can only come for real when mankind faces nakedly, as never before, the true perpetrators of their subjugation from within and without. Help Nefertiti to remember. Her vision has the potential to map a point of origin charting the topography of women who have chosen to align with the fortunes of the power elite. Their minds, no longer their own, reflect the division, fragmentation and distortion held beneath the surface and passed off as normalcy across lifetimes. Women who have not owned their soul, women who have left their morals behind and what they know to be right. Face what you perpetuate."

It was then that I heard the queen whisper "You are of my lineage." "You carry the potency of force most like mine and abused it as I did. Lifetimes of selfishness have cemented you into my mold doctor. For both attributes you are sought."

"Why am I sought?"

"Look closely, sister, we were needed. You and the other women he and his kind have pursued, hold the key.

Visions engulfed me. Sludge swallowed up my mind with dark molecular configurations. I was there with women like myself allowing myself to be frozen in the deep freeze at the Ground Goddess Café.

I saw a global psychic pollution, equaling any environmental toxicity threatening the planet.

"Your early abuse this time delivered you back into it and set you up to be a channel." Gary murmured. After a long meditative silence he spoke again "Your life has been perfectly orchestrated in the negative right up to your finding Shemura. People don't phantom these kinds of synchronicities but it is the only way to end them." He responded, his voice slipping away.

For the next three days I lay as though I were in labor, rebirthing myself through this debasing brain sludge as it united gradually with the sea of ill spilt blood. I flet Gary and I both trapped within it, fearing at times I could not breath and would drown. The mad queen, whose life was tied to mine, fought against truth, as did I, while the beseeching pleas of women and children tugged at us, like an undertow.

"Take heart, daughter of tarnished light. When this is over you will begin to move in reality, for the first time in thousands of years, towards the light. A few women willing to live through this kind of experience will begin to clear it and make it easier for those who choose to follow."

Then the Earth bathed me in a luminescent peace. The cave hummed with tones, both delicate and serene, calming even this dirtied, frustrated, seafarer. I heard music and was sure it was the Earth's song vibrating through the cave continuing to grant me a reprieve from torment. Her love drew in help from the stars. Swirling galaxies of prismatic light made rainbows to comfort and encourage me. Within her tranquil beauty I slept, amazed at her mercy, dreaming of being swept away in feelings of joy and wholeness. I don't know for how long I rested only that I was awakened by the coyote's call and as I opened my eyes I felt her spiteful breath before me. She glared that hateful, mad grin. I was back 3500 years, alone again with the queen of Egypt.

Chapter

23

Stealing the Moon

Act II

Scene 3

[Nefertiti squats by the blood red River Nile. It has become a hellish sea of imprisoned souls.]

Nefertiti: Go home doctor. Let us call an end to horror. I have not the heart nor the memory for more prodding. Remember me to Shemura. Now say good-bye.

Natalie: Good-bye? Without the answers that brought us all this way? You cannot mean this, queen.
Nefertiti: Let the world dream on, searching for the missing Nefertiti. Go home.

Natalie: You have been here all my life. Now at this moment, when you promised to reveal what has brought us all this way together, you say go home?

Nefertiti: Yes, yes, go home. I cannot pass through this barrier. I am in the sarcophagus that loving a madman has sealed me within. Look at this heart. [She tears open her garment to reveal a metal plate, strapping her chest in tightly. She beats on it, shouting.] Inside here is your last scene. Break this belt and you can have your final mystery.

Natalie: With what currency can I buy back my soul from this hellish sea?

(From out of the sea, ravaged priestesses of the ancient goddess cultures come crawling to the shore near our feet.)

Chorus of Women: Now listen to our blood sea queen. We are the women who through birthing the race of men wed our force with all life. You and women like you sold us to power. We are food for your pharaoh. His condemnation of women unleashed armies against us to guarantee our fall. See us now, for we are lost from your history books. Once we were holy women. Our lives were lush with a culture woven from tenderness and wisdom. We fled injustice as our temples were burned, our babies murdered and worse. We did not give in easily. They portrayed us as the devil incarnate, then crucified us for hundreds of years across the continents, or forced us to mate with our captures to avoid being slain. We were more than murdered, we were made impotent, silenced from effect, our imprint erased to shape civilization. We died choking with memories that tied our truest motives to unspeakable horror. When women contemplate returning to the fullness of their being these memories return to stop them. They see our vaginas dragged from the hooves of faceless horseman from your Egypt across Europe, through the

192

Middle East. With each woman blocked from returning to her essential nature we continue to be held in bondage. Help us now, queen of Egypt, release them, reveal the secrets of the dark priests temple.

(Nefertiti is distracted, turning to hear the cries of her daughters. She rocks, holding her head.)

Queen Nefertiti: I feel nothing. Why are these women strangers to my heart? Their pleas refract off dead metal. Where have I lost the key to unlock love? My heart is blank. It will not let me respond to their pleas. Find a way doctor, break me open.
[From the bottom of the Nile a flowering lotus plant rises. Images unfold as the petals float one by one towards us.]

Natalie: Come, queen, messages surface from the source of all that is. Come look here, tell me what you see.

[Nefertiti returns to the water's edge, then turns away.]

Natalie: Do not abandon truth, now, queen. We are so close.

Queen Nefertiti: Where do I find the fire of desire that is no more? Nothing in me wants this.

Natalie: You were once revered as a goddess of great light. The Divine Mother is still within you. Break power's muzzle and it is yours to live again.

Queen Nefertiti: [Looking deeply into the first lotus flower as images unfold] Taris, my darling brave daughter, why do you cry out from this lotus? Is that I by your child's bed? [She wails] I ignored your blood stained sheets soiled by his seed.
[She turns away]

Natalie: Let her show you now what you refused to see. Let the pain break your heart open if it must. Great strength demands great pain. Let Taris pull you from your husband's jaws.

Queen Nefertiti: What woods are these that ring out with my grandson's cry? Blessed birth, let me hold our baby boy. He has my eyes, alert, vigilant. When did I fall asleep? What is this filth? This infection pouring from your thighs? Oh, mercy fled, you birthed your son in river mud to hide him from my husband. Frightened, laboring alone in the cold Earth, too weak to call for aid. Lovely Taris, you shivered dying with fever, your breasts too infected to nourish our boy, I was told it was the fever that took you from us. They hid this from me and I had not a mother's instinct to find your truth. Where have I squandered the inborn knowing to protect you?

[There is no reply. Nefertiti reaches out as the body of Taris and her grandchild float away from her on the river of blood, then we lock eyes.]

Natalie: Does your heart now return queen? [Nefertiti shakes her head. She closes her eyes] Look then. Here is the second lotus petal.

Nefertiti: Soul sickness returns. With it the blindness I allowed to consume me. There is no love here. I am falling from grace with what I do not do. Life abandons my flesh. I perish with the neglect I cast my daughters into.

Natalie: Look a second time into the lotus flowers. Fight against oblivion, queen, you are my last hope.

Nefertiti: Nerfernefertatun, your daughter Mora, here she is. What beauty, we have given birth to twice. Elegant with the grace of an elk, Mora, my swan bubbling with creativity, turning the world merry, telling me with her smile there is hope. Nerfernefertatun, let me fill my mother's heart with love for you. You were once so very proud, tell me you found a way to save yourself from him, the pharaoh whose light sought to freeze you in gray ice. (Looking deeper, she sees it is not so. Crying) Nefernefertatun, you used your beautiful agility defending yourself against your father's sex. You turned yourself fallow living out your days, dabbling on the periphery of your genius, to deaden yourself and hide from his lust. Oh child, you ran from the deep river of your feelings but it did nothing to stop him. He is upon you sucking your virgin blood. Here it is daughter, you vowed to outwit him by sealing yourself behind a wall made from incest's mortar. And I have poisoned you further with my hatred of him. The line blurs between my hatred of him and all men. The confusion scrawls into you daughter. It is passed down. This is how we tie you to him still. And you doctor, your hatred and neglect have delivered her to him again, but she can make it still. She tires of hatred's drown. She has found Shemura, the love goddess. Her seeds of consciousness are deep within our child and so planted will sprout. Tell me this is all, that I thithed no more of this hell to my own children.

Natalie: Do these revelations break you from his curse?

Nefertiti: No, no, no! There is more! I dredge the bottom of this river sludge, here is the eel I have become.

[Sheeh's image comes into focus]

Nefertiti: My precious Sheeh, your Shemura. Here they come, Tatut and Sheeh, two lovers matched with the rarest of complementary strengths. Allowed to unite in purpose, two cosmic warriors of the highest rank, they will bring us the world's transformation. Their bond was life's gift to return us all to the temple of divine lovers. Joyfully, playfully, sensually, and yes, sexually we could climb with purest intent the internal ladder to our highest divine natures. She and Tatut would bring back the love goddess. They had it all to resurrect the innocence of desire. She was the bridge to clear a path for love to strengthen for all humanity.

They were to inherit our world leadership. But I am a fool of revenge. I do not see Sheeh and Tatut were meant to be these lovers, these models of sensual redemption. I rage over Akenhaten's unstoppable sex with our cousin. Losing my mind to it, I do nothing to help my daughter or my nation as he manipulates Tatut away from Sheeh, out of sight. He castes his spell on Tatut's mind, confusing him so completely he looses himself and marries Sheeh's younger sister, robing Sheeh of her destiny.

Oh doctor there is more! Years pass, Sheeh's health deteriorates. She lays dying, her broken heart draining her of the energy to keep up the physical fight. It is then my Akenhaten performs his black magic ritual to keep her his for eternity. As she expires he cuts off her hand. He takes this piece of her flesh, like Seth's Osiris, then hides it from her so she must remain fragmented from herself lifetime after lifetime. He allows his most beloved aspirant, Sheeh to suffer the most. My only baby who dared stand against him. His magicians are clever and diligent, she lost the ability to heal herself. He leaves her so. The madman expects this will win her back. He disables her from reuniting with the damaged pieces of herself. This is his way of keeping the lovers apart lifetime after lifetime so he can have her for himself and stop loves return. Over and over again she works to break his hold. Still he tries to get her for himself, this time, through you. But this time he has not succeeded.

Sheeh has become Shemura and with her blessed relationship to life has developed her work, found her hand and united with Tatut again. Her genius has brought us her work of feminine intelligence helping many to heal including herself. She has regained her immortal soul. She lives firmly alive in her consciousness, present for us all, igniting humanities prayers for wholeness in each monent. And, she has brought you to me. Now I give you what ties us together as one. Our plots will no longer imprint the collective mind. May this truth be your fire burning all restraints. Come see what has became of your beautiful one, your beloved Nefertiti, Egypt's queen of the sun.

Scene 4

[Nefertiti walks into the Nile and I follow her. Underneath its waters a great door opens. Inside is a chamber where Akenhaten and his priests perform their rituals of magic. Nefertiti's spirit is summoned. We watch as they evoke her desire for hatred and revenge drawing the queen under the control of Akenhaten's hooded priests. She lays herself on the pharaoh's obsidian bed. There they encircle her chanting, filling the room with blackness.]

Queen Nefertiti: False Pharaoh of the people, of the source, of cosmic light. This is what your people did not know about you. I let you tie my hands with the rope of my own hatred, my legs with my willingness to be blind to the plight of my own daughters need, my hips with the selfishness to love a madman who has taken the domain of manifestation from the goddess in all women. Your priests pelt me with frequencies of sound that their science knows will grow my negativity huge. I abdicate responsibility and abandon my own flesh. Dismembered from my body, you Akenhaten take charge of my divine essence. I let myself become your captive. You need this women's womb, this, my potent erotic force, you use. You who have been life's abuser are cut from the mother's magic by your own brutal actions. Now you are tied to us women with more need than you ever fathomed. How dumb negativity is! How stupid, to have let you take me with it. I gave you use of my women's talents to serve you. You send me out on this reddened sea of the collective mind to harvest souls who are flailing in unremitting pain. You feast on their energy for your psychic survival. I have learned to seduce the innocent, to thieve their energy laid open to me like oysters to be plucked. Helplessly they writhe before me, no match for our insatiable need for energy, nor for my prodigious talents. I am your fisherwoman sucking up the soul meat from these sad unconscious waters, stocked with human suffering. I am more mad with hunger each time I allow this. As life flees from me I, like you am left in fear and frenzy and so,

I do more for you, bring more of them to you. As we earn our obscene immortality it goes on this way for centuries. Armies lead by madmen feed our dark power. What would we do if mankind were free of misery, Akenhaten? We, and those modeled from our imprint would starve. You would no longer be able to caste your rod hooking the vulnerable, nor could I pull in your catch. When did I forget? It is this we do, as mankind agrees to separate conscious from unconscious, we hide in the deep shadows.

Husband, bankrupt violator of life it is at night I hone my skills. It is the dark I love, when you send me out in dreams to harvest the wandering emotions of those broken with pain, poverty and subjugation. I work for you gathering up the women and children's dissociated KA, their divine essence, as they break with pain.   Frustration rises on tidal waves of wronged lives. Here we have our feast! My expertise drains the fury off the rotting carcasses of women's stolen divinity. The blood sea of the goddess slain is our hunting ground. The sea of unmanifest dreams, of stifled potential, the squandered sea of the feminine captured, where the souls of children die alone, abandoned, utterly hopeless. Here our supper awaits. You cannot do this without a woman like me and so you make sure I will always be remembered as your brightest light, to cover up for your lack of equipment, your impotence, your inability to move energy, as only a woman can. I am your fiend, your addict, living off the catch of power's ceaseless unbound net.

[Akenhaten is carried towards her.]

Natalie: How is my madness linked with yours? What is this energy of perversion I have spawned all my life? Show it all to me queen.

[The queen takes off her gown and lays out beckoning her husband to come to her on his obsidian bed]

Queen Nefertiti: At dawn you come to me Akenhaten starved, hungering to reap the energy of my nightly harvest from my womb. It excites you that I am stanced against nature, armed against life, filled with those whose energy I steal and let you enslave. And finally you are mine alone again. It is I you want to sex now. I have found a way back to your favor. Here is your power supper. Humanities soul ingested is then spun back to them a reverse spin of artificial intelligence, masked as reality. We manipulate their unconscious! You need them to live a half waking life to continue your vampirization of their souls, their energy is your psychic blood. You make sure their connection to the Divine Mother life is perverted by our rituals. This is our control! I am their dark birth mother, pregnant each night for you to empty me of my sick meal. With each heist I have grown more addicted to being used. Life embraces me no more. Each passing year I grow less able to tear myself loose. When I beg you to help me remake this hideous thing I have become, you say it is my hallucination. You send out waves of priests to remake our image in artificial light before the world. Lies charade as reality down the generations to keep us fed. Who would believe me husband when I tell them that the body of the beloved Nefertiti, coregent to the great inceptor of monotheism is your whore, your secret weapon, that our lives, famous for dedication to the highest human aspirations, in the end served only this dark powers endless appetite for destruction? Who would believe us doctor, that your world, thousands of years hence, would be riddled with secret controllers beyond borders addicted still to our secret rituals. Their raging wars are ours and our descendents feeding frenzies, satisfying the insatiable hunger of a dark immortal power elite. Our menu, wars with schemes of genocide, decades of disasters, engineered diseases, the perpetual illusion of scarcity. It has grown a momentum all its own, a rolling stone tearing the tubes from the guts of humanity, like kidney stones breaking open the collective urethra. Don't you see doctor? It has escalated beyond anything good-hearted men or women know how to stop. The warm of heart cannot fathom our cold bloodied agenda. It is too terrible, to hideous to face, to see. This is how our dark power remains virulent. The roar of our thievery rumbles inaudibly throughout the modern world. Your New Agers want to love us. Fools! We will never stop ourselves. We count on the fact that no one can hear, see, or believe what we do to them. We have strewn the future minds of men and women with macabre venues of desecration and perversion, increasing our numbers while diminishing humanism, generation by generation. Our acts against life reproduced as normal behavior have created men and women without human feeling or conscience. As the sensations of being human are deprived, future generations have been as you say doctor, 'dumped down' to mask our plot. Our agents are the killers, drug addicts, thieves in high and low places that roam the slumbering streets. Child abusers darn the robes of holy men because of us. We will never stop. There is nothing for us but to go on. We and those like us cannot feel, cannot be intimate, and cannot live in the present. We are all allergic to life. What is there left for us but to keep on with it? You ask me doctor, how is our madness one? I have let myself become no more than his empty channel his vampire and you dear doctor you are my progeny.

Scene 5

(In the final days conspirators from the old regime that wish to reinstate Egypt's god's and goddesses threaten Akenhaten's life. He disappears bargaining from a concealed retreat. The people are told he is too ill to rule. In a move to maintain his power, he gives consent for Nefertiti to rule Egypt in his absence. I help the mad queen prepare herself from her cell for her reinstatement as the Great Queen of Egypt. I watch as her appearance is restored to fit that of a pharaoh. Turning from her mirror her painted eyes glare piercing the theater with remorse.)

The Pharaoh Nefertiti: History remembers Akenhaten as the bold renaissance heretic king, a unique hierophant of the Aten, a bearer of light and now finally, for all the world to see, a lover of women. After all, look who he made Pharaoh!

In the end I was Egypt's beloved queen again. By then I had only one love. I loved our dark power. Its madness has made it simple to care about no one, therefore to feel nothing of what we had really incepted for the world. Cold calm has become my only comfort. When asked to return to rule how could I resist? His scavenger given unlimited resource. No one would suspect I proceeded Medusa strapped on to the masthead of his nation's ship, protecting his pirated place in history. Now I have it all. I am back, my beauty restored, heralded as a beloved queen of light, a star in Egypt's heaven, an ascended master, a phenomena, a resurrected miracle. A woman at the helm of the Great Egyptian Empire! My bust will adorn the necklines and mantle places of women across the globe for thousands of years. I am a model, a women who rose to the top of an enlightened culture. My beauty and power became renown. It was I, Nefertiti, who became the administrator of his ideas, I who carried forth his renaissance in art and culture, I who upheld his laws. It is I, Nefertiti who assured his one Father God would be forever whispered on dying men's lips, fighting each other in His name. It is I, Nefertiti, who with my husband, stole your moon, your being, your love, your goddess. It is I, your beloved Nefertiti.

THE END

Chapter

24

The play <u>Stealing the Moon</u> opened two months later on the full moon. Inside, the newly built auditorium smelled of freshly cut pine and cedar mixed with the aroma of rose amber and cigar smoke. Dozens of golden gels set off the royal pair in a blaze of artificial light. As the actress playing myself prods Nefertiti for the origin of her madness, the audience is held in an uncomfortable and questioning tension.

Thinking back, I am surprised how open to the play's performance the staff at the Shambhala Lodge had been. They had even helped me to find semi-professional actors from a local community theatre. I did not understand why they pulled out all the stops, advertising the event on the Internet. Later, on the local evening gossip show, to my horror I found my play billed as 'the never before disclosed sex lives of two of Egypt's most renown queen's, Nefertiti and Akenhaten.' The auditorium was swarming with vultures and doves.

I had not imagined from how far they would come to silence this revelation until I spotted the gold leaf initials O.R. etched on the brief case of Omar Reinwalt, head Egyptologist for the Berlin Museum. As the performance began, the spotlight reflected off the coned headdress of Nefertiti. I caught a glimpse of him. He was an official, heavyset man seething from this heinous attack on history. Flanked on his sides were officers from the occult society that kept Akenhaten's vendetta alive today, cloaked in a school of metaphysical studies. They were scowling in the darkened room, scratching rigorously on tablets lit with hand held laser spotters. Another woman was stomping on the sanctity of the disciples of the One Father God. Was this why Shambhala made sure we played to a sold out house, so that the world press could tear apart the piece, sure to be reviewed as a flagrant and unsubstantiated attack on the founders of all patriarchal religion? I caught sight of Yogicar, with his arm around brethren of the old mystical order, and I trembled. I reminded myself that this was all I had to give to women, starting with Yogicar's innocents. And what of the children today whose energy was being held hostage? What of Gary's sacrifice? And Shemura's commitment? All the acts against her that Akenhaten created, and I perpetuated, through many lives, had to stop. I resolved not to bring down the curtain prematurely but I was frightened.

I sat in the wings, dizzy and nauseous in my director's chair, unable to focus within the cacophonous energy that swept up from the chastising mob. Then rising up from the genuine seekers in the audience another wave broke loose. Through the gentle, pulsing flow of their sincere desire for truth, I saw her. Shemura walked to her seat in a cape of translucent aquamarine, embroidered with a white triangle. Like Moses, she parted the Red Sea with her beauty. Her presence lent strength to the seekers, sabotaging the blanket of suppression that threatened to engulf the theatre. Yogicar's women turned their heads in acknowledgment.

I sat back feeling the plays intent and significance break loose. It began to penetrate the atmosphere through the opening her love created. I was relieved, knowing she had by now read this manuscript, which I had mailed to her.

Afterwards, as the crowd dispersed, I made my way through the ring of women that surrounded her. Janis and Charlotte wanted to be introduced, and they in turn brought their friends in to shake the hand of the woman who was "good all the way through."

I had hoped that the performance would cause great change in these women, and in myself. But I felt no startling metamorphosis as I bumped the shoulders of the theatergoers while making my way towards my mentor. Yogicar shot me an icy stare, as did the other well-dressed professionals elbowing their way out. They were talking into tape recorders and cell phones. I wondered what repercussions my expose' would unleash, but more than that, a feeling I could not shake troubled me, Gary was still here.

After we embraced, I asked Shemura if she would step outside. She nodded yes, while holding the hands of the girls as we said our good-byes. She suggested we meet away from Shambhala. I offered to take her to the center of the vortex, out by the triangle of pyramids. She agreed, and as we drove away in Shambhala's van I could not rid myself of the feeling that Gary was with us. We walked together, the harvest moon dwarfing the three pyramids. I asked her about Riley, her children and her research. She did not cover-up the pain, disruption and injury I had brought into her life.

We stood at the apex, two women who could not be more opposed in nature or intent. She was the white goddess; soft, present, and balanced, the genius of woman. I was her enemy.

My heart broke with remorse. This women had to be one of Divine Mother's rarest of pearls, a gift wrought from extreme love, pain and dedication, a beacon for humanities rebirth. I had done nothing up until now but search her out for destruction.

There were not enough tears to wash clean what I had done to her, while pretending, even to myself, to be a sincere seeker of truth and enlightenment.

I wept with the pain she bore at my expense and begged her to tell me what I could do, at this late stage, to improve her life.

" Fully broken hearted and shattered, you can now fan that tiny flame within you, yearning to grow a heart. Don't give into the despair, the depression or the pain that will come your way as you try to make this right for the future, Natalie. You have gone through a great deal to surface this." She said softly.

"I heard Divine Mother speak to me in the desert." I responded. "She said this would end when I have given back in equal measure the love I have conspired to destroy.

"Yes" she answered, "and don't forget, you're not the only woman compromised unknowingly by a hidden evil. Experiencing the deep shadow self can unblock the valves of even the darkest heart. With this process of raw naked change there is fresh hope for addicts of every kind, to free themselves. You'll find a way to help many others. It will not be the same journey as your own. But your work can be a mirror to surface the unique relationship others have to their own deep shadow self. It is time for us to work together, to do something that has never been done before."

As she reached for my hand, I felt her immense force. I, too, had this force within me. I had chosen to use it wrongly, but its potential was equal to hers.

We held hands; stretching like a tightrope of dark and light across the event horizon, ready to affect this moment in time with our united knowledge.

Before I could voice my gratitude, headlights came from three directions; one speed to the canyon's western rim then halted abruptly, the other snuck behind a thicket of pines, dead in front of us, and the third stopped and started, in menacing fits, until it flanked the eastern rim. They had us encircled. She was used to being watched, stalked, hunted. Like trumpets heralding Akenhaten's curse from the past Men had always dropped their net of terror around her. It had been that way for as long as I had known her. Now their familiar threat of retaliation came at us from the three directions as it so often does when women gathered with the hope of creating real change. I feared that I had once again fulfilled Akenhaten's will, bringing her out here, but she only laughed. Pointing to the pine-rimmed road, illumined by the full moon, we watched as the desert wind spat mouthfuls of sand onto the three vehicles watching us from above.

"You know vortexes and me" she smiled. "We'll have the time we need. You've done very well, Natalie. I felt the truth in what I saw tonight. I know what it takes to surface these kinds of revelations and present them to the world. I commend you for your effort." She spoke, covering my shoulders with a magnificent black cape embroidered with a symbol that resembled the opening to the 'Cave of the Womb' When a dark sister holds her deep shadow before us, white sisters everywhere can begin to forge a path out of the curses of the past. And, your dark sisters will be able to release enormous trapped energy. Natalie, I believe there are many more like you waiting for a way to release the energies that bind us all to the mistakes of the few. The history of the formation of our psyches has always been controlled by a few self-aggrandizing people, who let their own desire for power or revenge mar the lives of us all."

"Shemura, even as I sought to uncover the roots of my destructivity, I contributed to the death of a beautiful young man." We stood, our capes phosphorescent in the moonlight, while I told her the story of Gary, the man who would have allowed me to birth the goodness of my female spirit had I let him, and what I did to derail his efforts.

"Yes I remember him from your manuscript." she responded. "He has not been released." I told her. "It didn't work. We had hoped that the play would free him and the children."

"And you too?" She asked.

"Yes, and me too."

"The play moved you out of the jaws of Akenhaten to the beginning of your freedom, to this place where we can work together." She said, closing her eyes in deep contemplation.

"Isn't there anything I can do? Is it too late? Without him I could not have finished the play."

"Yes there is something we can do." She responded stretching her arms out, causing her white triangle to glow with the moon's opal light.

She described what she felt.

"He is here with us now." As her words filled the valley the coyotes barked and the undulating bodies of the rainbow dancers rode across the sky, taking shape in the slow moving clouds that swept in front of the mammoth smiling face of the moon.

The chanting of Akenhaten's monks came, then faded as the laughter of the rainbow children and the elderly showered us from the spidery web of spiraling stars.

I watched her face melt with the ecstatic pleasure of a woman making love. Her love drew Gary's spirit into her body. She moved like an ancient dancing goddess, a candelabra strobbing the canyon with a thousand rays of crystal light. I stood beside her, my light flashing in petulant flickers. I was filled with remorse for what my actions had created, deeply grateful that Shemura was coming to Gary's aid. She could undo the damage I had done and free his beautiful soul, but I was also jealous as I looked at her pleasure. She was making love to my lover and even though I had tossed him aside, it hurt me.

"Your love is not strong enough yet to do this for him" she said.

"Your play moved him. He is no longer trapped with the unloved children. He is in a kind of limbo world. He wants to speak to you."

I looked up, shocked, and then shook my head in agreement.

Shemura broke into laughter " He's half in my body and half outside. He wants to say something to you."

"No wonder you were addicted to her, Natalie" Gary said as clearly as if he were standing beside me. She's every bit as amazing as you said. It's like entering that Parish painting, you know, the one with the ecstatic woman stretching to kiss eternity on the edge of the world. She's all feeling, like the tenderness of a golden morning light, the excitement of vibrant cobalt blue, shimmering with compassion inside the purity and warmth of a sexy tangerine heat. It's so beautiful in her, I don't want to leave!"

"He has to let go, tell him, Natalie. My love is here for him so that he can let go. He needs to let go into the light. Tell him." she said moaning, her arms still moving like a swaying Palm in the moon's light.

"Why does he need me to tell him?" I asked, my voice still tinged with jealousy and possessiveness.

"Because it is you he is really holding onto. You and this place, his home."

The illusion that she was taking him from me clouded this new insight and I could not feel, at all, that his desire for me was holding him to this world. I was faced with how far I had yet to go.

"Your attachment to him is making it harder for him to let go, Natalie." Shemura exclaimed softly.

My tears wet the neckline of my cape as I released the dreams we shared. Dreams I shared with Nefertiti and her love of Akenhaten, along with dreams of heroic transformation and mutual love, shattered in betrayal. I felt Nefertiti with me, her yearning for resolve and healing melded with my own. Shemura's love and unflinching support for me all these years, her mentoring, as I surfaced the deep shadow had allowed me to break through the stiff linen of my mummified heart. I felt Nefertiti's sobs of gratitude reverberate in my heart as my tears fell unto the parched desert floor. The miracle of our united healing, in parallel realities, through this one woman's love, parted the clouds that had obscured the moon. A sea of luminous light united us all as women. My heart was inseparable from the fallen queen's.

A divine mercy engulfed us. We soared with the hope we had destroyed in many others. Our sobs of remorse, birthed by the grace of Shemura's love, were returning us to the threshold of a potentially compassionate life.

"Is this what Jesus had in mind when he said, "Love your enemies?" I asked her.

"Female intelligence, emotional intelligence is rooted in practicality. If this is to end, it must end in love. But without experience of the deep shadow it becomes impossible, a farce and a repeating cycle of delusion."

I felt a gentle kiss, like the wings of a butterfly brushing my cheek. I knew Gary had let go with the help of Shemura's love and it had freed him to move on.

We sat in silence, with respect to his passing, and then she asked me,

"What is it that you need from me now?"

"Gary and I had hoped the play would release the children whose energy is still trapped in the unconscious. We were hoping it would dislodge the dark power's hold on Yogicar's women and many others."

"It will take more than one performance to change what has been in effect for thousands of years. This is only the beginning of understanding what has been hidden away in the divisions of the self."

"How will it happen?"

"The children will not be entirely free until humanity grows an awareness of their deep shadow self and with it an awakened heart deep enough to forge open the gates of unconscious control. Only then will the reign of invisible terrorism end. It will change when people begin to pull off their blindfolds and see that we have all been captives in the prison camps of internal power. Then one person at a time will unlock the depths of compassion that will make the change possible and irrefutable. Dawn is quickly approaching the darkness of humanity. The energy from the potential and memory of when power stole the moon mutating our feminine natures can now be transformed. "You are going to keep writing aren't you Natalie?" Shemura asked. "It is time for us to write the next book together."

"Another book? On what?" I asked.

"You can re-write this one, you and Nefertiti, healing every error, liberating every wrong choice."

"How do you mean, change the past through writing it differently? How is that possible?"

"No, it is not possible to change the past, but you can resurrect the squandered potential of your loving soul, every aspect of your self that has been numbed by your wrong choices and those of others toward you, the energy that has been lost, stolen darkened and trapped. You can rebirth your loving feminine potential into the eternal present."

"Through writing?"

"Yes through re-writing your life. We've been working intensively in this area recently. We're finding the transformation of the soul has been unending. We're calling it <u>Righting Our Lives</u>."

"<u>Righting Our Lives?</u>"

"Yes. Think of your life as a ship out at sea, on course to actualize your hearts deepest dreams, sailing to realize your own unique contribution to the sacred journey of humanity. Life meant for you to fulfill your own unique course, your destiny, joyously, in harmony with life's purpose. That means all your talents, your abilities, every blessing and challenge were designed with intent. As you made wrong choices and others interfered, your potentials were weakened and you became trapped. Your vessel veered in another direction. <u>Righting Our Lives</u> self corrects that detour from evolution, returning us to that original potential. We each have a glorious, loving destiny to fulfill. That is why the mother of all life birthed us here. It is inscribed on each of our DNA, but its script has been overwritten. Like a ship with a broken rudder, you were sent in another direction. Now can be your turning point, now you can right your life by correcting those decisions, miasmas and circumstances that pirated your voyage."

"You mean I can rewrite every wrong turn?"

"Yes, every major turning point. Life wants us to restore our deep energetic connection with her, to heal the severing that has allowed all this enormous cruelty to repeat and grow more potent, generation after generation. Now is the time to retrieve our energy from the unconscious, to deeply feel and know our path from the inside out. It can only truly happen when we have our own authentic energetic selves grounded in our bodies. First that means experiencing the deep shadow for what it has become. Only then can the authentic self be truly free of the programming of the past."

"Does everyone have to go through what I've had to in order to discover their deep shadow?" I asked her.

"No, that's rare. Most will find the map home far less convoluted. Most will find the deep shadow layered in hereditary programming. It won't be as tough but it must be experienced first hand for any kind of enduring integration or lasting inner peace to occur. With all the prophecies of a New Age, nothing is going to truly change much unless this is done. Each person needs to know this event from the inside. There is no easy way and there is no alternative course. History has always repeated itself because the roots of darkness are not fully experienced without guilt or shame to the depths necessary for real transmutation. And as far as the New Age goes, most of what is out there is a packaging of a portion of truth, a marketable portion that allows the so called enlightened leaders to avoid facing and transforming their own deep shadow. It's just an unconscious manipulation of those naive of the dark side for profit and control. The oppressed after every uprising have always become the oppressors.

Start with yourself Natalie. This is your opportunity to no longer be trapped in the negative, as you have been lifetime after lifetime, repeating the vendettas and compulsions of the power mad. This is the lifetime when it can truly end for you. You won't have to hunger for my destruction the next time around if you follow this through, you'll be in a whole other frequency; not the frequencies of power or control, but of love.

Righting our Lives will help you to reconfigure your relationship to the negative and positive collective it is a conscious act of liberation, of breaking your contracts with power."

"How did you discover it? "

"It was given to me through intuition, through my direct relationship to life. Everything that has ever really worked for me has come that way. The greatest healing is the simplest, you know that. You're going to be amazed. The new energies coming into earth now make it much more direct than ever before. People are ready for this. I can feel them, Natalie, groups all around the world, especially women, desiring to end the abuse of power, and men willing to do the hard work of inner cleansing, to support them. There is no time to waste. Life desires the rebirth of humanity, she is leading the way.

I heard Ruby's words "Da mama bring him in and da mama will take him out" and I was back in the 'Cave of the Womb,' the force of the Earth's creative fire burning through me.

Through Shemura's words of encouragement and inspiration, and in the face of her beauty, I could feel the deceptions moving through me. I still felt diminished. I know I too am beautiful, she has taught me that, but it is still cloaked in stealth, in my addiction to power. I have chosen to grow my power, to become some kind of mutation of female desire. The Earth now is showing me a legion of greedy and captive women in the shadows just behind me. I sense looking at the Great Mother's face beyond the fire I must not stop here. I feel Earth yearning for me to complete this work with Shemura.

About the Author

Sienna Lea is an author who lives in San Diego's North County. She wishes to make herself accessible to you as you respond to her work. Please communicate with Sienna directly by visiting her website at: www.SiennaLea.com or email her at:
transformingearth@yahoo.com

To obtain information on attending or arranging a *Shadowland Seminar*™ please visit the website. Seminars will be posted on the website as they become available.

For Aysha Loves gifts and tools to assist in the transformation of consciousness including: books, tapes, creative projects, events and seminars please contact:

Sensorium at www.Aysensorium.org

Righting our Lives™ Intensives will be posted as they become available.